I0551733

Ray Bradbury's

PLEASURE
TO BURN

Selected Stories from the 2019
Literary Taxidermy Short Story Competition

Edited by

MARK MALAMUD
and PAUL VAN ZWALENBURG

PLEASURE TO BURN

All stories © 2019 by their respective authors
Introduction © 2019 by Paul Van Zwalenburg
Afterword © 2019 by Mark Malamud
Anthology © 2019 by Regulus Press
Cover art © 2019 by Lamour Feu

First Regulus Press printing November 2019
Signal Library 10-9102-42-90

Regulus Press, Seattle WA
www.regulus.press

All rights reserved. All characters and other entities appearing in this work
are fictitious. Any resemblance to real persons, dead or alive, or other
real-life entities, past, present, or future is purely coincidental. This book
or any portion thereof may not be reproduced or used in any manner
whatsoever without the express written permission of the publisher,
except in the case of brief quotations embodied in critical reviews.

ISBN: 0999446263
ISBN-13: 978-0999446263
(Regulus Press)

OPPORTUNITIES FOR
FUTURE TAXIDERMY

"In my younger and more vulnerable years my father gave me some advice that I've been turning over in my mind ever since. So we beat on, boats against the current, borne back ceaselessly into the past."
— F. SCOTT FITZGERALD, *THE GREAT GATSBY*

"One beast and only one howls in the woods by night. See! sweet and sound she sleeps in granny's bed, between the paws of the tender wolf."
—ANGELA CARTER, "THE COMPANY OF WOLVES"

"How had they met? And he would go out like a light."
—DENIS DIDEROT, *JACQUES THE FATALIST*

"A purple ocean, vast under the sky and devoid of all visible life apart from two minute ships racing across its immensity. I am so happy to be homeward bound, and I am so happy, so very happy, to be alive."
—PATRICK O'BRIAN, *THE WINE-DARK SEA*

"We went to the Moon to have fun, but the Moon turned out to completely suck. Everything must go."
—M. T. ANDERSON, *FEED*

"She enters, deliberately, gravely, without affectation, circumspect in her motions (as she's been taught), not stamping too loud, nor dragging her legs after her, but advancing sedately, discreetly, glancing briefly at the empty rumpled bed, the cast-off nightclothes. Perhaps today then … at last!"

— ROBERT COOVER, *SPANKING THE MAID*

"I know your sleep is precious. A warty angler in your pants."

—CHOO 3T FISH, *"BLOOD IS BLUE"*

"My name is Laura Palmer, and as of just three short minutes ago, I officially turned twelve years old! I have to be numb."

—JENNIFER LYNCH, *SECRET DIARY OF LAURA PALMER*

"The child's world changed late one afternoon, though she didn't know it. In a while she would follow."

—NICOLA GRIFFITH, *HILD*

"The past is a foreign country; they do things differently there. But I didn't, and hardly had I turned in at the lodge gates, wondering how I should say what I had come to say, when the south-west prospect of the Hall, long hidden from my memory, sprang into view."

— L. P. HARTLEY, *THE GO-BETWEEN*

It was a pleasure to burn.
↓
When we reach the city.

— Ray Bradbury, first and last line from *Fahrenheit 451*

CONTENTS

Introduction

Welcome to *Pleasure to Burn*, the anthology that collects the twenty-one prize-winning stories from the Regulus Press 2019 Literary Taxidermy Short Story Competition.

Wait—literary *what?*

Is this really a collection of stories about the art of preparing, stuffing, and mounting the skins of animals? Or are the stories themselves dead—with only the illusion of life? Who wants dead fiction lying around their house?

Well, here's the thing—these stories are *not* about taxidermy, and they're certainly not dead. In fact, you might go so far as to say these stories bring new life to lines that otherwise have become moribund from years of over-familiarity. You see, every story in this book started from the same prompt; and it was the job of every author to bring that prompt to life.

The idea of writing prompts isn't new. Writers have been playing with varied techniques for years. But this particular take is unusual—and unusually compelling—and its name, "literary taxidermy," coined by my friend Mark Malamud, does a wonderful job of capturing the essence of the process. It involves removing the "insides" of a well-known fictional work (short story, novella, or novel), leaving just the surrounding first and last sentences, and then "re-stuffing" that shell with a new story, a wholly-original narrative that, by taking over those beginning and ending lines, creates something unique, personal, and often surprising.

And here's another thing: the original work remains untouched. You can still go back and reread it any time you like. Which is great, because after reading some of these 2019 finalists, you just might want to revisit the original to remind yourself of how it was stuffed. You might want to do this because the stories in this anthology are nothing like their source, taking unexpected turns that may amaze, humor, and sometimes shock.

A few years ago Mark and I experimented with literary taxidermy (not yet given that name) when he and I were doing some writing exercises together. The beauty of using a pre-determined start and ending was that we were able to jump-start our exercises, forced off the starting line by the starting gun of someone else's first line, and left to run, however we chose, toward someone else's finish line. How efficiently, how creatively we managed that run was revealed by how well our re-stuffed stories worked.

Sadly for me, even with those predetermined start and finish lines, there were no guarantees of success. I wasn't, in other words, much of a literary taxidermist. Mark, on the other hand, managed to come up with more than a few creative and interesting stories he could mount on his writing wall, so to speak. Or include in his book *The Gymnasium*, a collection of nineteen stories written between 2003 and 2017 that "re-stuff" classic works by Milan Kundera, Thomas Wolfe, Ian Fleming, and others. Even though I wasn't much of a literary taxidermist, I had a lot of fun during the process. And I'd gotten some writing done, which after all was the original goal.

Since that time, Mark has gone on to publish not only *The Gymnasium*, but also three fabulous anthologies from the 2018 Literary Taxidermy competition, and he had so much fun doing so that he encouraged Regulus Press to run the competition again this year.

The 2019 Literary Taxidermy Short Story Competition used first and last lines from *Fahrenheit 451* by Ray Bradbury, inviting writers to stitch together their own stories using those opening and closing sentences. Which brings us to this present anthology, which contains the finalists from the

2019 competition. Each and every story in this book starts and ends *exactly* the same way, and while that may sound repetitious or boring, in fact it's part of the fun. Seeing just how each author moves from beginning to ending is eye-opening, and mind-opening. Every story here is unique, and a lot of fun to read: despite sharing a common frame, they are all very *different*.

The stories in this collection range from funny to disturbing, with stops in between. Some are just plain strange. (I mean that in the best possible way.) They cross genres; they cross continents and cultures; they cross worlds as well; and they vary in style, voice, and tone.

The authors are eclectic, too. They range in age from twenty-one to sixty-five. They also live around the world, so you're about to read stories from the United States, Canada, Australia, New Zealand, Cyprus, Singapore, the Czech Republic, and the UK. The winning author in this year's contest is **Cuifen Chen**, a student in Singapore, working towards her MA in Creative Writing. Her story "Sunshade, Starlight" is an impeccable example of literary taxidermy. It embraces Bradbury's first and last lines to create a seamless and perfect-fitting narrative between them.

But there's more to these stories than the pleasure found in their distinctions or differences. Their similarities can be just an intriguing. Common themes stood out, some surprising, others maybe not so much: witches burning, photographs burning, post-apocalyptic worlds burning, fires intentional and accidental and blue, sunburn, and myths of creation. And yet even when stitching up a story with a common trope (say, burning witches), these authors fashioned something distinctive. And that's the wonder and beauty of the human imagination, that it can take the same beginning and ending, and make something of its own.

This second year of the Regulus Press competition reaffirmed many of the first year's discoveries, and that pleases me. The stories in this anthology were selected anonymously by me, Mark Malamud, the editors at Regulus Press, and a panel of eight professional-writer judges. After each story, you'll find a short biographical note about the author that may (or may not) give you insight into how the story came to be written.

Reading through this collection gives you some sense of the breadth of creativity of literary taxidermy. It may even inspire you. Go on, give it a try. Experiment with first and last lines of your own choosing. See where they lead your imagination. And maybe submit a story to next year's competition!

Paul Van Zwalenburg
08 September 2019

Kit Carmona

The 9000th Loop

IT WAS A PLEASURE TO BURN.

I'd stoked the fire blue—hot enough to crack skin and boil blood. When I turned my hand over, I could see that the heat had melted the fat of my palm, which bubbled up from the rifts between skin char-dried to leathery plates. Fat doesn't burn hot, but it does burn high and bright.

"Doesn't it hurt?" Iska asked, and I almost laughed.

"Of course it hurts."

The first time I thrust a fingertip into one of my fires, I thought I'd finally died and gone to hell. The heat was an alive thing, feral and furious; it dug teeth like jagged razors into my flesh. I yanked my hand back, sure I'd never try that again. But convictions don't last in this place.

"Then why?" she asked again. I looked sideways at her, surprised at her persistence, and found her studying her own palm. Perhaps she was worried that madness was catching.

It didn't surprise me that she couldn't understand. Iska had taken to this place more easily than I had—maybe because she was younger when we were taken, or maybe she had always been more flexible. Even when I was young, I was resistant to change. I wept when I graduated primary school, and I wept when my mother met her second wife, and I wept when she decided to move us off-planet, even though mother said that the colonies were as verdant as the Earth a hundred years ago, and anyway, all I'd be missing was blighted grass and desert dust.

"It's nice…to affect something," I explained, and Iska

nodded wisely. She could understand that. Sometimes I caught myself thinking that she had the wisdom of a far older person, before I remembered that she *was* older. Iska wasn't 18, not any more than I was 26. Or if she was, she'd been 18 for longer than most people get to be *anything*.

The fire was creeping up my arm now, hot on the trail of the melted fat that dripped down my forearm like clarified butter. *Shh*, I told the corner of my mind that gibbered and flailed against the pain, and thrust my arm into the pond.

Once, on our six hundredth loop, I let the fire take me whole. Iska told me later that she'd found only a grease spot and flour-fine ash where there had once been muscle and bone and hunger and desire. But it made no difference. I woke up in my bed on the six hundred and first loop with nothing to show for it but a lingering sense of unease and redoubled dread at the sorry state of our mortality.

I wished I had my pocket knife, the little stone one I'd labored over in our twentieth cycle, when we were still trying to figure out what they wanted us to do. I'd even engraved the blade, ingratiatingly hopeful that they'd let me keep it. But of course it was gone come morning. Also gone was the fat round blister on my thumb, and the little line I'd sliced into my palm when my hand slipped on the blade.

They didn't let us start a loop with *anything*, not food or clothes or tools to hunt with. Not that it mattered if we caught anything, really. It's not like we could starve in the 12 hours before the next reset. It was just something to do.

Iska theorized that they were studying human advancement—that they wanted to see us discover the wheel before the cart, and to hunt with sticks and rocks before we learned the trick of bows and traps. If we could make a fire, we could make a forge, and so on. But I don't think they expected me to get so stuck on fire.

More fool them. Fire was everything they'd robbed us of: cause and consequence; growth and death and decay. It was inherently transformative, nature's original alchemist. It was the only thing in this whole damned bubble that was as hungry as we were.

(I didn't really buy Iska's little theory. Doesn't advancement rely on your ability to build on the last day's labor? Can you ever progress, if everything you've ever made unmakes itself overnight? But I didn't contradict her. There was no point in it.)

"Can I try some?" Iska asked, eyeing my smoking hand, and startling a genuine laugh out of me. I hadn't laughed in a hundred cycles—not since the first time we reached the edge.

"Sure," I told her giddily, and held my breath before snapping off the brittle tip of a blackened finger. My nerves were already char-broiled: I felt nothing.

Iska gnawed at it thoughtfully, savoring the smoke and the sinew and the barbecue-crisped edges.

"You burned it," she criticized faintly, and I guffawed.

"Sorry," I snorted. "I'll do better next time."

"You *won't*," she corrected. "Next one's mine."

We took turns deciding what we'd do with each loop. There were a few hundred cycles where we went our separate ways, but if this place was claustrophobic with a partner, it was downright suffocating alone. And anyway, we always started out in the same room.

On Iska's days, we did a lot of walking. Sometimes she muttered to herself, tracing invisible lines down her forearm. When I listened, I mostly heard gibberish: "The herd, 34-75," she'd murmur, or "Inlet B, 80-85." But I rarely listened. To have interest, you needed hope.

"I'll do you one better," I offered, counting backwards in my head to maintain my composure. The pain was unbelievable. "I'll give you the rest of today."

I don't know what made me say it. Perhaps it was the look on Iska's face: open revulsion and traces of fascination, but mostly just *boredom*. Perhaps it was that Iska had surprised me today, and I wanted to do the same. It couldn't have been curiosity.

"You mean it?" she asked breathlessly, and I nearly smiled as I nodded. It was remarkable, really, her ability to work tirelessly and utterly ineffectually for years and years of the same day. I envied her naiveté. If I was her age when we awoke here, still ripe with plans for a future that had not yet taken shape, maybe I'd be more like her. Maybe.

Iska was scratching some numbers into the ground, muttering all the while.

"What are you doing?" I asked finally.

"*Shh*," she hissed, and kept working. I shut my mouth, sat on the ground and tipped my head skyward.

There was the cluster of cumulonimbus, a familiar herd of thick-furred sheep, chasing the sun west; and that wispy, indecisive streak of cirrus had cut only halfway through the sky—so it was noon, or perhaps 12:30.

At 3:00 or so in the afternoon, those great fat gobs of hard-edged, billowing rainclouds would converge in the center of the sky. At 3:15, lightning would rend their bellies open and water would pour down in sheets. It didn't faze us anymore. The floodwaters washed east-southeast to funnel into a great earthen basin. By 4:00, the skies would clear.

"Okay," said Iska.

"Okay?"

"Okay, I'll tell you what I'm doing."

She pushed her hair back from her forehead, tucked an unruly lock behind her ear.

"I'm doing a census," she told me, and I choked on another laugh. Two in one day: a new record.

"A *census*?" I asked, incredulous. "Of what?"

"Everything. Everything in here with us, I mean." She chewed the end of her hair thoughtfully. The last time Iska explained one of her schemes, she'd looked self-conscious—embarrassed, even. This time, she only looked distracted.

"Everything like…?"

"Every rock, every tree…every geological formation. I have them all written down."

"Written *down*?" Notes scrawled in the dirt or carved into a tree wouldn't outlast a reset.

"In my head," she said impatiently. "Obviously."

I blinked at her in disbelief. Our prison was miles across.

"I'm looking for a pattern," she continued. "I…" she trailed off, screwed up her forehead. "Let's take Herd B. The cattle closest to 0,0—the resurrection point," she clarified. "Every day they travel west, chasing the sun. But Herd D, by the plateau, they go east—for exactly as many miles in the opposite direction. Do they remember, like we do? Are their movements a habit, or an instinct, or an instruction?"

"I—"

"And east of the floodplain?" she continued, as though I hadn't interrupted. "There's a waterfall that's exactly as high as the basin is deep. Oppositional forces. Between them, a kind of symmetry."

"Symmetry," I repeated, instead of laughing in her face. It was hard to believe that she was still trying to make sense of this place. It had been nine thousand loops since we first woke up here. In all that time, nothing had ever changed.

"And then there's us," she went on, and then hesitated.

"Us?" I echoed sharply.

"Never mind," she attempted, but I was a dog with a bone.

"By all means," I drawled, "tell me about our *forces*. We're, what, tall and short? Masculine and feminine?"

"No," she said quietly. "We're—progressive and regressive."

"Excuse me?"

"The harder I push toward the horizon," she said, still looking away, "the deeper you dig in your roots."

"My *roots*?" I didn't need to take this. "Iska, I'm sorry to rain on your little project, but you're being more than a little delusional."

"I thought you'd say that," she said softly, with disinterest. It was—disquieting. The last time Iska and I had fought, she shrank to a tenth of her size. Now, I couldn't seem to touch her.

"Nothing *changes*, Iska. Of course the cows go the same way every damn day, because it's the *same day*. And I won't blame you for going a little bit mad, but—"

"We're not," she said.

"Not mad?"

"Not living the same day."

"*Excuse* me?"

Now I was angry. Living a Sisyphean nightmare is one thing. Living a Sisyphean nightmare and being told that you're *not* is quite another.

"I'm not saying there's no reset," she explained quietly, and I settled down slightly. "I'm only saying—you're projecting a little."

"I'm *projecting*?"

"Because you won't change."

"Because *I* won't…?" My charred arm throbbed. "The world undoes everything we've ever done and *I'm* projecting? Nothing *changes* here, Iska!"

"I have," she told me softly, and I closed my mouth. Because she had, hadn't she? She spoke quieter now, but with conviction. She did not wilt in the face of my anger. She watched me burn my hand alive and asked for a bite.

Iska's eyes studied my face. Was she taking notes? Would she hold this in her mind? How did it all *fit* in there?

"I remember everything I've ever seen here," she explained calmly, eyes fixed on mine. "I remember the first loop, and the second, and the fifteenth, and the fiftieth. And so will you, I think, if you try."

Of course I remembered the *first* loop. And sure, I remembered the second—naked again in spite of the clothes we'd struggled to fashion from the great fat leaves of the tree near the cave. But the fiftieth? The five *thousandth*?

"You haven't been keeping track," she sighed. "You won't know the numbers. But the second time we trapped that ox, how did you screw it up?"

"I cut into the stomach," I answered automatically.

"And the day we washed away in the flood, what did you pick up?"

"That little gemstone, the—"

"And when we first saw the edge?"

"Enough," I told her, flushed with some emotion I didn't quite recognize—disorientation? Humiliation? "I get it."

"You think we're frozen, but we're not," she explained softly. "We're not in cryo, we're in a damned growth chamber. You're just determined not to grow. Now come on. You said I could have today."

I followed wordlessly.

The little wisp of cirrus had nearly dissipated, and the cumulonimbus was swollen fat and dense as a mountain. Oppositional forces? I shook myself off like a dog, briefly forgetting my injured arm, and swore as an entire plate of burnt skin *cracked* under the strain and dropped to the dirt with a *pfut*.

There was something wrong with the storm cloud. It looked—darker than it should. Something acrid and sour rose in my gut. Gods, the pain in my arm should have plateaued by now, but instead it built and built. I bent over a tree stump and retched.

"Something's different—"

"No," Iska said coldly. "It only feels that way. That's good, though."

"Where are we going?" I gasped, coughing, and she cast a sly glance in my direction.

"We're going to see the edge."

My stomach sank. I'd only seen the edge once, and I swore I wouldn't go back. It was too much, too hurtful to know. The first time we saw the edge was the first day I gave myself to the fire.

Back then, we still thought this place went on forever. We didn't know if we were the only ones lost in time, or if the rotation of this whole world had stuttered like a scratched record. Every day we walked as far as we could in a new direction, before the day's end picked us up and dropped us back where we started. Until the day that we hit the edge.

There was—it's hard to say—a sort of *shimmer* that bent the light; made the grass on the other side warp and twist and sway. There was a shuddering of sound, a thrumming reverberation of wind. And beyond it, the world *whirred* with change.

As we stood frozen, buildings rose and fell and rose again. Impossible fractals as long across as city blocks bloomed from dry earth; they thrust themselves skyward, and they crumbled, and still more alien geometry sprang forth in their place. Perhaps there were people—there were blurs of motion, sometimes, near the edge—but they were too fast to follow; or we were too slow to keep up. Life went on without us.

"What will you do?" I asked Iska, between gritted teeth. My jaw felt tight.

"I don't know yet."

"You don't—!"

"The last time I saw it, I…knew less," she explained smoothly. "I didn't have enough data. I wasn't ready to see the city, much less draw any salient conclusions."

"And now?"

"Now what?"

I resisted the urge to roll my eyes. "Now you're ready?"

She shrugged, infuriatingly frivolous. "I don't know," she answered. "If I'm not, I'll learn from that too. But we'll find out soon enough," she added, and actually winked. I felt faint, and furious, and nauseous, and maybe just a little bit curious. "We both will. When we reach the city."

"The 9000th Loop"

KIT CARMONA is a freelance copywriter in California, in the United States. They are a disabled, nonbinary writer who uses fiction to explore dysphoria, discomfort, and disconnection. They are currently writing a fantasy novel about the identity-shattering process of losing their mobility—but they swear it will also be a fun, magical romp. "The 9000th Loop" is their first published short story.

They say: "My story is about feeling stuck. It's about rejection, and failure, and the incremental successes which ultimately prove nothing and change nothing. But it is also about the danger of getting lost in that feeling. It's personal—isn't writing always?—and I hope that you enjoy it."

Justine Frakes

Scattered Ashes

IT WAS A PLEASURE TO BURN. It really was. Comparatively speaking, there are far worse ways to go. So many women having left this world with water filling their lungs. You never forget it…their fearful eyes meet yours as they go under. You can't look away. Waiting and watching as their last breath bubbles to the surface. Then the water stills. There was something so final about it, the dark water silencing their cries and leaving no trace of the horrors that had taken place. Not until their bodies were retrieved. And since they drowned as they should have, their innocence was restored, though their lives were not. It was far better to die innocent than to live accused. At least, that's what they say to comfort the families.

Even if Elise had a family, they would receive no such comfort. Her fate had already been decided, no tests or trials were needed. She was a woman. She lived alone. And she refused the attention of men. She was guilty by default. Having seen these proceedings too many times before, she saw no use in denying it. Whether she was guilty or not, she would pay for her perceived sins.

When they came to arrest her, she asked them if the shackles were made of iron, and when they said they were, she decided to make a show of it. They wanted to burn a witch. *So she gave them one.* The moment they touched her skin, she screamed and writhed, acting as if she was in terrible pain. Perhaps she heard it from some fable or old wives' tale, but it just seemed like the right thing to do. Through her feigned howls of anguish, she caught a glimpse of fear in her captors' eyes, and a smile crept onto her lips. *These men who believe they rule the world—they fear me!* This euphoria was swiftly followed by guilt. *Who am I to put fear in the hearts of men?* she thought. Women and children for miles around feared these men, it was expected, a part of life. But it did not make it right.

By the time they got her outside, it seemed the whole town had gathered to see the commotion. Most were angry and hungry for vengeance; but as she looked through the crowd, the faces of her friends, their grandmothers, mothers, and daughters stuck out. The mix of emotions she saw reflected in their eyes was overwhelming. Terror, sadness, disbelief. A spark of an idea flashed through her mind. *Until they strike the match, I'll turn my pyre to a pulpit*, she thought. They would never listen to the words of a woman. Even if she speaks the truth. But they would hang on to every word spoken by a *witch*.

Perhaps they too were startled by the numbers that had gathered, but her captors were caught off guard enough that for a moment she was able to break away. The crowd jumped back, giving room for her performance.

"Do you have any idea what you have done?!?" she snarled, daring anyone in the crowd to meet her gaze. "This is *my* town. I am the only witch that has ever resided here and so it shall remain till my blackened heart crumbles to ash! And even then, from beyond the shroud of death, you ne'er will be rid of me!"

Someone shouted, "What about Ruth Solomon—she was a witch!" Elise turned towards the voice, and the crowd parted to reveal the fool who made the mistake of believing anonymity would keep him safe. She felt a rage beyond her years bubbling up inside of her.

"You know *nothing* of witches," she hissed, stepping towards him. "Ruth was no witch, anyone with half a brain could see that." She turned back to the crowd. "How many innocents have you killed in search for the real thing? Ten?

Twenty? You have condemned others to die over sins far less than you yourself have committed!"

She searched the crowd, locking eyes with anyone who had had a hand in the deaths of innocent women. "I know the god I hail will thank me for my services. Can you say the same of yours?" She could taste the fear in the air. Hearing the guards behind her, she turned on her heel to face them. This was it. Her last chance.

"Now hear me, and remember," she shouted, turning to the rest of the crowd, trying to keep her voice from cracking. "Tell your children—and tell your children's children—the signs. Witches are not young girls or old maids as your stories have told you." She lowered her voice to a growl: "We are *beasts*. The only true way to test a witch is with iron, it burns our skin." A gasp rose from the crowd as she held up her wrists, bruised and bloodied from her theatrics. "True witches cannot cross a patch of daisies, and children who wear chains of them will be safe. Hang them on fence posts and doorways, all within will be safe from witchcraft." She hesitated a moment, catching her breath. "Plant them by a witch's grave and she cannot return." Determined looks passed between members of the crowd, and it gave her a small sense of peace, that even if she died a villain in their hearts, she, and all those burned before her, would have flowers on their graves.

The guards found their courage and grabbed her shoulders, trying to drag her from the crowd. But she wasn't done yet. She threw herself to the ground; and kneeling, she closed her eyes and said,

> *"As above, so below.*
> *This town shall reap this curse I sow.*
> *From winter's thaw until time's end,*
> *This town, no witch shall come within.*
> *Through ashes, smoke, and pyre burned.*
> *On my grave I shall return!"*

Her words echoed through the silent crowd. There was no doubt in their minds that she truly was a witch. She ended her speech with a blood curdling howl that came from the pit of her very soul. Perhaps it was a trick of the ear, but all who heard it could have sworn that a chorus of voices joined in that ungodly howl. As her parting bow, she rolled her eyes back in her head, and let herself slump to the ground. The town was silent. No one moved. No one breathed. She could feel all of their eyes on her. The guards eventually came forward again, and gingerly picked her up, more out of fear than kindness. Her head was pounding with all the thoughts racing through it. *Where did that come from? Will this change anything? Was it worth it? Maybe I was possessed….* The righteous anger began to wear off and the seriousness of her fate seeped in, like water filling the lungs. All she felt now was tired. Once the guards unceremoniously dropped her in her cell, she rested her fevered cheek against the ground, then succumbed to the cool darkness around her.

Elise didn't expect to make an impact, but as they shackled her to the wagon that would take her to her fate, she saw the whole town outside, planting daisies. Mothers and fathers working side by side in their gardens, older children patiently teaching their younger siblings how to make daisy chains, or how to braid them into hair. With everyone outside and the sun shining just so, it was difficult to believe what awaited her at journey's end. A part of her wished it would happen here, surrounded by people she cared about. Even if they felt nothing but hatred for her, it would be a small comfort. *But that's what I get for making such a big show*, she mused to herself, and the city, a day's ride, offered a much better audience, anyway. They had a few 'witches' already and planned to make a day of it, one right after the other.

The sun felt warm on her skin, but she couldn't stop

herself from shivering. The stern, silent driver of the wagon glanced back at her.

"I know what you did."

Somewhat surprised, but no longer afraid to meet a man's gaze, Elise looked him in the eye. "What do you mean?"

"You're no witch," he said, turning back around, "but you are doing the right thing."

His words hit her like an arrow. For days she had stayed strong, held her head high and refused to let the hatred under her skin. But this…these simple words of kindness, of belief—a sharp pain echoed around her chest. Her throat burned with words that she could not say, and her vision began to blur from the tears that threatened to flow. Hearing her choked cries, the driver softened his voice and spoke over his shoulder. "If there is anything I can do for you…just let me know."

With a trembling hand she wiped away her tears and looked at him, this man that she did not know, that believed her. Over her shoulder, she caught the last glimpses of the town that never believed her as a woman. Only as a witch. She looked ahead at the simple road lined with trees that filtered the sunshine as it fell on the path. She closed her eyes, listening to the creak of the wagon's wheels, the soft methodic thud of the horse's hooves, and the far too steady beating of her own heart. She opened her eyes, sighed deeply, and lay down, gently adjusting her chains.

"Wake me up when we reach the city."

"Scattered Ashes"

JUSTINE FRAKES is a full-time office worker and part-time artist in Kansas, in the United States. "Scattered Ashes" is her first published short story.

She says: "In too many stories and too much of history there were limited roles a woman could play: daughter, wife, mother, widow, witch. And while a woman is so much more than those roles, those in a position to write history tend to place women into those categories. I wanted to tell the story of a woman who takes back the narrative."

Marie Wilson

Violette Aubergine

IT WAS A PLEASURE TO BURN. The magazine clipping of Lana Turner crackled and curled like a strip of bacon, her shapely gams sizzling in the flames. My uniform, on the other hand, just smoldered, kind of like Lana in *The Postman Always Rings Twice*. I poked at the garment with a stick and suppressed a cough as my life went up in thick, toxic smoke.

That melting blob had once been a regulation leotard of psychedelic purple, a day-glo colour invented for Jimi Hendrix. The shade is also known as phlox, after the flower, but Danny used to call it statutory grape. I denounced his quip as off-colour; he replied that it was just a little black humour. Danny and I used to crack ourselves up sometimes.

Figure Fabulous, the exercise salon where I'd been bouncing around in that phlox leotard for the last year, resides in a strip mall in South Vancouver. The salon announces itself with a sign that glows royal purple against grey concrete, and its interior looks like a Belle Époque bordello or a phantasmagorical dream straight out of the summer of love: a riot of purple in every shade.

Up until two weeks ago, Danny and I were living in a small off-white apartment above a store on Broadway. "I'm on Broadway," I wrote my dad when we moved in, despite knowing he wouldn't find my little joke funny. Dad always said that the reason my mother left was to become a star of stage and screen. And there's nothing funny about that.

Mom ran off to join the circus a dozen years ago, just as the sixties kicked in. I was eight. From then on, Dad raised

33

me on TV and TV dinners. I liked old movies and turkey the best, with *Bewitched* and fried chicken running a close second. Two years ago I moved out of our bungalow in Kitsilano, and so Dad put in for a job transfer. When it came through, he moved to Toronto.

Dad's in paint. Well, not *in* it, it's his business. From an early age, I learned to read by sounding out the fanciful names of the paint colours in his sample books and fan decks. I love books of all kinds now, but whenever possible, I still like to dip into the colourful poetry of a fan deck.

At first, I thought my mother's sudden absence was a puzzle to be solved, like a Nancy Drew mystery. Once the case was cracked, she would reappear. But one day I came home from school and walked straight into her closet and just stood among the clothes she'd left behind. I knew then that she wasn't coming back. I buried my face in a blood-red summer frock and howled my loss to its empty bodice.

Before Mom left, Dad used to bring home colour swatches and stir sticks for me to play with. After she left, he no longer brought anything from work except his defeated old self.

La Belle Époque was also known as The Mauve Decade because of the popularity of that shade among artists and fashion plates. This purple passion actually began in 1856 when a teenager serendipitously invented the first synthetic dye. A brilliant purple, the dye was christened "mauve," and became all the rage. But because it faded so easily, mauve is the word we now use for pale lilac.

By the time I was ten, memories of Mom were fading fast and she was being replaced with movie star moms. Around that time, I went to see a new release called *Madame X*. In my child brain, I conflated actress and character and my mother. I became convinced that Lana Turner/Madame X was my mom. And she was wonderful—although abused by a slimy playboy then banished to wander lonely streets, she only pined for her child: me. I cut out a picture of Mama Lana from a magazine and kept it in my box of treasures.

Danny and I used to have morning coffee at the Black Cat Café just down the block from us. Then I'd catch the bus to go open the salon and Danny would head upstairs from the Cat to attend courses at Harmon's Business College. I used to imagine that his classroom was the sort of dull place Laura fled from in *The Glass Menagerie*.

Laura was among the monologues I'd been working on with an idea to audition for the two theatres in town. I didn't have a clue how to go from high school ham to real actress so I started reading books about method acting. Plus, I'd seen movies where young nobodies became bona fide thespians: *A Star is Born, The Actress, Stage Door*. They all travel to New York or L.A. for their big break. Toronto always sounded like the city for me to realize my dreams.

But that was out because Danny said he wouldn't come with me. He thought my aspirations were unrealistic and stupid. I wanted to show him he was wrong and to convince him to make the move to my Emerald City. So I devoted myself to perfecting my skills in secret. Every evening, when the last patron went home I'd draw the mauve salon curtains and turn the lights down low. Then, in the dimmed amethyst blush, I became Esther from *The Bell Jar*, Mary Queen of Scots, Laura.

Scents of sweat and perfume lingered in the air until the vibrant smell of fresh oranges overtook all. You see, Esther tells her story about "the summer they electrocuted the Rosenbergs" while peeling an orange. The fruit is not in the novel, but aside from helping to lift the monologue off the page, this bit of business provides a physical focus, which is supposed to help short circuit nervousness during performance.

For Laura, there was no fruit involved but rather the Method technique of "substitution," wherein you substitute someone from your own life for someone in the play. Pick the right sub and your performance will come alive. For Jim, the Gentleman Caller, Danny was my stand-in because he used to make my heart sing, just as Jim elevated Laura with his kiss. But, also like Jim, Danny could just as easily break the horn off your damn unicorn, just zap the magic right out of your life.

It was that same zap-the-magic thing that also made Danny the perfect substitute for Elizabeth I, Mary Stuart's archenemy. Whenever I'd say Mary's line: "In myself, I know you to be an eater of dust," I'd picture myself standing on the real Broadway under a marquee with my name on it. And Danny would be standing before me, only he'd be about twelve inches tall. Looking back on it all now, I don't know why I ever wasted a moment on that miniscule moron.

One day a couple of weeks ago, my manager told me to go home at lunch because it was a slow day at the salon. I ran to catch the bus, hoping to meet up with Danny on his break at the Cat. Pushing open the glass café door, I spotted him in a round booth across the room. I was aware of a lightning quick movement by his side, a blurred impression of someone rapidly exiting the booth, an amber flash.

Just as rapidly, Danny rose to greet me and steer me outside. I glanced back at the flash: vanishing into the powder room: saffron hot pants bursting at the seams. Outside, Danny lit a cigarette and talked fast about nothing. My eyes followed a wisp of smoke up to his soft, chestnut hair then further up to the neon sign of a black cat wearing a top hat.

Eggplant is a shade of purple named for a fruit. The colour is more commonly called by its French name: aubergine, which I think is the start of a good stage name. A lot of fruits lend their names to the purples—mulberry, beautyberry, plum. The latter is also an adjective meaning prize, as in "plum role"—and that is exactly what I had an audition for at the Arts Club Theatre a few weeks ago.

I wore a vintage black velvet dress to highlight my prop. The dusty black theatre floor around my feet was littered with fragrant peel once I'd uttered Esther's final words. I thanked the director and made a hasty exit. Outside, the naked citrus got juiced in my fist as I released all my pent up nervousness. The next day I was back weighing and measuring and recording results on individual lavender charts: pounds and inches lost and gained, the ups and downs of these women's lives.

"Make sure that eighth of an inch is legible."

"Yes, Mrs. Zailo."

"The last time I tried to read my chart the numbers were all scribbles."

Monica Zailo. Angular. Severe. Rich. On that day, she'd brought her stepdaughter in for the salon tour. Coifed and polished, Tiffany Hull wore designer jeans and a constantly amused smirk. She looked like someone I knew or had seen in a dream but I didn't know who. I also didn't know what she found so amusing.

At tour's end, I moved in to close the deal. But my sales patter just bounced off the orchid walls, for Tiffany, it turned out, was underage for signing a contract. "And," she apprised me in upper crust tones: "I'm not that interested in belonging to the salon." As I walked her to the door, her stepmother swooped in and brushed me aside. Arm in arm, they made their exit. I watched them cross the parking lot, thinking Tiffany really could've used a membership, or at least, a bigger size of jeans. Her smirk, more than her butt, brought out my inner cat.

And then it came to me.

"Can I help it if her mom belongs to your salon?" Danny protested. "Tiff and I are classmates, that's all."

"Well, if that's all, then what was *Tiff* doing smirking around the salon today with no intention of joining? Who does she think I am? And who do *you* think I am?" Suddenly, I had an image of the two of them, lounging in a Cat booth, smoking cigarettes and roaring with laughter at the girl in the statutory-grape leotard. The thought cut into me like the sharp blade of Mary Stuart's fate.

The next morning, Danny wasn't speaking to me. I tried to put a happy face on at work but it didn't help that at lunch I phoned the theatre only to learn I didn't get the plum role.

Bruise should be a colour name but it would never fly in a fan deck—no one wants to paint their room such a painful shade. But my heart was feeling the intense deep-purple-blue of a fresh bruise. I told my manager I had a splitting headache because you don't get to go home for emotional contusion. On the bus, I silently rehearsed apologies: "I'm sorry I mistrusted you, Danny. I have a rampant abandonment complex that causes me to get jealous and paranoid. Forgive me, for being such an insecure twit."

Back before the synthetic variety was invented, purple dye came from a species of sea snail and was so rare and costly that only the very wealthy could afford to wear purple. Hence, its status as the colour of royalty.

When I opened our apartment door, Danny sprung up from the couch like a jack-in-the-box. He rushed toward me, fumbling with his undone shirt buttons. Behind him on our couch: Tiffany Smirk, smoothing her dress. Danny stopped before me, hastily tucking in his shirt. Regret and desperation flashed into his poison-green eyes.

In a twinkling, I saw our year of love and laughter going up in sky-high flames—all the challenges and triumphs, the lovemaking and promises, now reflected back through a lens of scorching deceit. He looked like he wanted to beg my forgiveness but Mary Stuart doesn't suffer cheating playboys gladly, and her words left my mouth with assurance:

"God's spies that watch the fall of the great and little, they will find you out." I backed him into the room, a fury mounting. "I will wait for that, wait longer than a life, till men and the times unscroll you, study the tricks you play…." He opened his lying maw to speak but I struck like a bolt of lightning: "My heart beats blood such as yours has never known!" As he fell onto the couch next to his cowering dream secretary I turned on my royal heels and departed the dungeon.

Heliotrope is a bright violet colour named for a flower. The word is from the Greek: *helio* meaning sun, and *trope* meaning turn, because heliotrope flowers are said to track the sun's motion across the sky.

I gave notice at the salon. And for the next two weeks, my nighttime crash pad was a beautyberry exercise mat. While my ex was in filing class one day, I went home to get my velvet dress and a few other things. My last night at the salon, I made lavender confetti of Monica Zailo's measurement chart.

And early this morning, I torched Lana Turner and the purple leotard in a campfire at Locarno Beach. Then I boarded a train to the metropolis of my dreams, The Big Smoke. No more of this two-bit, two-theatre town for me, and no more eaters of dust. Swathed in black velvet and carrying a satchel of oranges, I'm tracking my own lucky star across the heavens. My dad will put me up till I get my bearings. And my citrus and I, we will audition our juicy little hearts out. When we reach the city.

"Violette Aubergine"

MARIE WILSON is writer and actor in Ontario, Canada. Her mother was the second daughter of Royal Wells Borden—bear hunter, beekeeper, and descendant of the infamous Lizzie Borden. Her novel, *The Gorgeous Girls*, is published by Harper Collins; she has published stories in *The Globe & Mail*, *NOW magazine*, and *Fireweed*; and she received Honorable Mention for a story in last year's Literary Taxidermy Short Story Competition.

She says: "Colour captivates me. It's integral to my photography and painting, and it crops up as a storytelling device in a lot of my written work. The fire-and-smoke palette invoked by the sentence *It was a pleasure to burn* got me started on my story, but then the setting took over—I once actually worked in such a purple palace. Hendrix would've loved it."

M. W. Philip

Let's Go, Cowboy!

It was a pleasure

To burnish your desire
With my fingertips

To polish your teeth
With my tongue

To beat the leather
Into submission

To go for a ride
To buck that boy

Into my home town
To slip on the saddle

Into bed unstable on the
Kitchen table in the back

Of the parking lot
Where tongue finds fingertips

Let's go, cowboy!
Every bump in the road

Is like rodeo fireworks
One hand at nine, one at three, oooh

What's the speed limit around here, anyway?
The road's not the only thing that's open

Wasn't that where we get off?
You know, forget it, just keep going

They say it's not the destination it's
The journey so don't even think

Of taking those hands
Off the wheel

When we reach the city

"Let's Go, Cowboy!"

M. W. PHILIP is a third-year graduate student at the University of Kansas, in the United States. His field of study is cognitive and perceptual psychology; in particular, he's exploring the relationship between color perception and emotional lability in prison populations. "Let's Go, Cowboy!" is his first published poem.

He says: "I grew up in Montana and have always been obsessed by the twin myths of the cowboy and the open road. This poem was my attempt to bring those ideas together."

Jennifer Smith

The Morning Stars

IT WAS A PLEASURE TO BURN.

When heaven cast us out, the air let us fall: feathers scorched, wings and bodies broken. I relished the memory of my father's angry words as he forced me to leave the only home I'd ever known. I feared separation, yet my spirit sang with freedom.

Unlike the mortals, born of earth and water, our father had created us from fire, the light of a thousand stars. I was the son of the morning, the bringer of dawn, and heaven echoed my song of reverence. Then came the humans. Father was enamored with his most recent creation. Fondly, he told us to watch them: "See, look what the man did today in the garden?" They were weak, helpless beings, though my siblings grew charmed by their unknowing. I played along, laughed and smiled, hoping to share in their delight.

I'd enjoyed tricking the humans at first. They believed any foolish thing I said. They would leap to follow any suggestion if there was a promise of pleasure or profit. It was too easy. I soon became bored. I yearned for someone to be my equal, a companion.

Father deemed my desires misguided. Then he cast me aside, unworthy of receiving his affection.

I burned with resentment.

And so I fell.

I took up my solitude like a cloak and wore my anger as a crown.

I watched, as Father had instructed. And I waited.

And nothing changed.

Last week I saw him for the first time. He stood among them, one human amidst a crowded marketplace, almost as rebellious as I myself had been in my younger days. Tables overturned. Doves fluttered in alarm as coins clattered against pavement. Shocked expressions and cries from onlookers. His eyes dark with righteous anger.

He was beautiful.

I begin to hear his name in hushed tones everywhere I go. I try to catch him alone, but he is always surrounded by hangers-on. Anywhere he goes, a crowd will gather. Ruffians and gentry alike, they all want to be near him. I don't blame them. His spirit is aflame with a heavenly fire. It shines through his eyes. The reviled believe themselves healed by a mere touch of his hand. Disease or demons, it matters not.

Being near him, hearing his voice, it is better than heaven ever was. Whether soft and comforting, or harsh with reprimand, I hang on his every word.

He goes sometimes to the mountains to escape the multitudes. Today he is alone, and I follow him. We cross the river, and trek up the narrow trail to the hills. My throat is full of dust. I should have planned ahead, brought water or a bit of bread to eat.

We reach the edge of the desert. The wilderness. I kneel down beside him and watch as he sits, silent and waiting. For what or whom? In my fantasies, I imagine he had noticed me among the crowds, had hoped I would follow him. And here I am.

I whisper, not wanting to frighten him. Or it may be because my throat is parched, but I sometimes tell lies to myself as well.

"Yeshua." His name is a prayer on my lips. His eyes open, and I let out a hiss of breath. I had underestimated the searing intensity of his directed gaze.

"Go away," he says. "I want to be alone."

"I don't blame you. Those people are irritating." I wave a hand, gesturing towards the city below.

"Hmmm." He continues to glare at me for several heartbeats, then closes his eyes.

"Why do you encourage them?" I ask.

"They are sheep needing a shepherd. Someone has to be the one."

He doesn't tell me to go away again. And so we sit in companionable silence until it becomes unbearable to me.

"You don't happen to have any water, do you? Or something to eat? I heard rumors you can do magic. Maybe you could turn that large stone there into a loaf of bread?"

"Don't be ridiculous." He laughs. It is glorious. I want more. I speak further nonsense, trying to make him smile at my ridiculousness.

"Go away, my friend," he says. "I'm trying to pray here, and you're distracting me too much." He closes his eyes, attempting again to ignore me.

He had called me friend. No one has done so in a long while. I watch my new friend in his meditation. I close my own eyes and wonder who or what I should pray to. My father? Hmph. That door closed long ago. Should I pray to any being who will listen? And for what? I want nothing more in this moment than the companionship—or dare I say love?—of this man sitting near to me.

And what does he want? I open my eyes, giving up on prayer, preferring to watch him. His lips turn down at the corners, sad and serious.

"What do you pray for?"

"At this moment? Peace and quiet."

"Then why do you bother with all those silly people in

the city? Do you wish to be their new king?"

"Of course not."

"I myself once thought that sort of thing was what I wanted. Before—"

His eyes glow with interest. "And now? What changed your mind?"

"You did."

He smiles again, and returns to his contemplation.

Warmth spreads through my limbs, my heart ablaze with it. The light and fire of heaven.

Home.

A flutter of wings and the faint sound of footsteps muffled by sand. I glance up to see my brother scowling at us.

"Michael." I greet him with a nod.

"WHAT ARE YOU DOING HERE?" His voice is the sound of thunder.

"Good afternoon, dear brother. Happy to see you, too. It's been far too long."

"Leave him alone," Michael says. *"He belongs to us."*

"Belongs to you? Last I heard, these humans were created with free will. Unlike ourselves."

"The will of our father is enough. It should have been enough for you. If you hadn't—"

"Shouldn't he have choices? Be allowed to enjoy the beautiful world that our father created for him, for all of them?"

Michael sneers at me. "You never thought it was beautiful before. What's gotten into you? What trick are you up to this time? I swear, Lucifer, if—"

"No tricks, brother. I have changed."

"We never change. We are eternally as Father created us. No choices, remember?"

"I chose to fall."

"Ha. You even lie to yourself. Father made you. He made you fall."

"No! That's not true, I wanted—"

"Enough. It is done. He is ours. Father has a plan for him. You need to stay away."

"Father—never mind. I don't wish to argue. I hope you brought him something to drink, at least?"

Michael looks a bit aghast, though he has no answer. My siblings tend never to think about the needs of the physical body. "What have you done to him?"

My brother always suspects the worst of me. "I've not touched him." I cannot bear to look directly at the object of our debate, his beautiful dark head cast down to stare at the sand, as if he can't hear our angry words. What must he think of our petty sibling squabbles? It is embarrassing for all involved.

A cloud of dust emanates from beneath Michael's foot as he stomps impatiently.

I sigh. "Yes, all right. I will go." As I stand, I force myself to look down at my erstwhile companion, now half in shadow. His head raised, his dark eyes bore into my own, and I imagine a flicker of sorrow there.

"For now," I whisper. I see his lips quiver at the edges, and I attempt a return smile and a cheerful, parting wave. "Until next time."

I then tear myself away and happily turn my back on my brother without further comment. Let him try his best.

And I will try mine.

The plan. Oh my father's plan.

Yeshua explained it to me, what Michael had shared with him in the desert after I'd left. It is terrible. I hate everything about it. And I don't see what good it would do at all.

We argue for days.

He is adamant. He would stick to the plan. My brother managed better than I to win him over.

I try to persuade him to run away with me. Somewhere my family wouldn't find him, though I know it is a lie. There is nowhere to run. Nowhere on God's green earth.

But he still has choices. Humans were created with free will. That was my father's big selling point when he told the rest of us about them. He'd given them the ability to choose their own paths. Five trees in paradise, and only two of them off limits. Stupid parlor games.

"Please just think about it," I tell Yeshua. "Consider what you are doing, and why. What good will it do?"

"I will save them all."

"Will you? All of them? You mean, everybody on Earth except for you? Because you will be dead."

He shrugs, as if that were unimportant.

"You will be dead," I echo. "And we don't know it will even work. We don't know what they've planned, beyond your pain and suffering."

"Michael said—"

"Michael repeats what he's told. He follows orders, like a good little soldier. Besides, he's been wrong before. When they told Adam he would die right away if he ate that fruit, it took him over eight hundred years. Right away, my—"

"My dear friend." He presses his fingers to my lips to silence my rage. I close my eyes, and lean into his touch.

"Please don't make it harder. I have to do this. I know it."

I kiss his fingers and he pulls them away.

"You sound like my brothers," I say. "Duty and sacrifice."

"Duty and sacrifice are sometimes all we have."

"What about love?" I ask.

"I have that, too. That's what it's all about, in the end. But sometimes we have to sacrifice everything for those we love." He turns to leave. His adoring fans await him.

Duty. Sacrifice. Honor. Love.

"To hell with all that," I say.

But I am now alone, and merely muttering to myself like a madman.

We are on the road into the city. Two days' ride. He has already sent some of his followers ahead, to make arrangements. Like Solomon the old king, he plans to make a grand entrance. Dazzle the crowds. It will lead to his death. He knows and he chooses it regardless.

He chooses death over me.

In the heat of the afternoon, we rest by a well. The mules need water. In the morning we will continue on our pointless journey. Knowing the end is so near, I don't wish for his anger, but I find myself arguing with him again.

I tell him how much I love him. Plead for all the other choices he could make. Choices we might make together. I run out of breath, as he sits there, silent and full of sorrowed determination. My chest hurts with longing to make him understand. To make him see the futility of everything in this mortal world, but also the infinite possibilities of life.

He reaches out, his skin is warm against my cheek. "Please, my dear friend. Let me do this. I must do this." My tears spill over his fingers as he gently wipes them away. "Do not weep for me. Let me remember your smile. But you must let me go."

I don't want to quarrel with him any longer, not now. Our time is running out. I swallow my words, my pointless attempts to persuade him. All my tricks are useless.

As they've always been.

The morning sunlight glints off the bridle of my mule as we ready ourselves for departure. We are close now. A ragtag crowd has gathered along the road, as usual, drawn to him like moths to a flame. The dawn is so gentle and lovely, it is difficult to believe in the reality of the promised violence to come. I close my eyes to savor the warmth on my face. I listen to the gentle murmur of voices that surround me as we follow the road towards the city.

I will follow him until the end. I will force myself to watch. Was this what my father intended for my punishment all along? Did he know this would happen? He told us to watch the mortals. Watching means standing by helplessly as they make choices that lead to their own ruin. Is this all part of my father's plan? Flesh and blood become food and drink to him. He toys with all of us, as pawns in a glamorous game. His marvelous experiment.

So I will watch. For once I will do what my father instructed. For the sake of love, I will do it.

I will watch my beloved suffer and die.

The crowds will be dazzled by his light, and then they will destroy him.

I will lose him.

And then I will be in hell once more.

When we reach the city.

"The Morning Stars"

JENNIFER SMITH is an interior designer in Virginia, in the United States. Her interest in comparative religion leans towards gnostic heresy and witchcraft, with a penchant for ancient mythologies. She has published a novel called *The Descent of Angels* and a non-fiction work called *The Fly in the Ointment: The Mysteries of Mary Magdalene*, and she received Honorable Mention for a story in last year's Literary Taxidermy Short Story Competition.

She says: "Upon reading the combination of *pleasure* and *burn* in the opening line of this year's contest, I immediately envisioned Lucifer, falling from heaven. In Christian tradition, both Lucifer and Jesus (Yeshua) are referred to as *The Morning Star*, yet they are considered enemies. I wondered, instead, what if they weren't? And what is the difference, really, between falling from heaven and falling in love?"

Stephen Yolland

The Hunt

IT WAS A PLEASURE TO BURN.

A good burn meant they would make shelters and stay awhile, with food and water to drink, near the banks of the big river that lay towards where *Walu Longu* slept every day, taking her flaming stringy bark branch into the dark till she returned the next morning to start another day.

A good burn meant they would stay long enough for his woman to safely birth his child. They would catch *jawan* and grill them on sticks till the scales and skin charred away and the sweet flesh flaked free, and all of them would eat till their bellies grew like a turtle's back, praising the fish for their generosity.

It was time they stopped. The old man was dying, of course. He would soon go and live for a time in the soul of *Anjea*, to wait with her until she sent him back to the earth again, and when he died his family would turn to someone to lead them. His family would turn to him.

He watched the old man struggle to keep his food down, walking a few paces behind them instead of striding out in front, and he saw the concern in his mother's eyes. He had thought about this deeply. He had seen twenty-two winters and summers, and he was ready for the responsibility.

As he looked across the forest as the flames he had lit took hold, he knew his brothers were on the other side, their spears ready, waiting for the *juwanbin* and *garril* to arrive, fleeing the fire.

The *juwanbin* would arrive first, some flying, and some—like the giant *nguyi*—running hither and thither in panic.

The men would concentrate on the *nguyi*, which they called "the racer" because it could run so fast. In their fear they could be herded this way and that, and brought down easily with boomerangs and spears, although some of the younger boys would compete to bring down flying birds as well, and probably fail.

And the *nguyi* offered them more than just its dark, sustaining meat, of course. The grey-brown feathers and leathery skin could be used to make a cloak that would last a lifetime and ward off the rain, and the bright blue feathers from their throat, prised for ceremonies, could be traded with other families for food or tools. The oil from their fat could be smeared on traps as bait, and the long tendons from their legs made excellent string. Their strong, rigid bones made knives that would last for years. Truly, the *nguyi* loved the people of the plain and gave them so much.

As a boy, the elders had shown him the first *nguyi* high in the sky over their heads and told him the story of how, in *Tjukurpa*—as his people called the Dreamtime—a blind man had lived with his wife in the bush. Every day his wife hunted for eggs for him to eat. One day, she followed *nguyi* tracks all the way to the nest. She found a huge bird there and threw stones at it to get at the eggs, but it ran towards her and killed her. As time passed and *Walu Longu* continued her journey across the sky, the blind man became hungry, and he worried about his wife. So he felt around the camp until he came across a bush with some berries on it and he ate some, for strength, and suddenly he could see again. So he made some spears and set off to find his wife. He followed her tracks and finally saw the huge bird standing by the body of his wife. So he speared it and banished its spirit to the skies, where it can still be seen in the heart of the river of stars stretching across the darkness to this very day.

Now, as the smoke rose, he knew that after the birds

would come the *garril*, hopping in their amusing, crouching way that the men honoured with their dance, and then they would stand and stop, looking behind them, as if waiting till the very last moment to flee the flames, for they hated giving up the protection of their forest despite the mounting danger. Only when their very tails were singed by the flames would they hop towards the half-circle of men, falling into the pits they had created and covered in rushes. And the men would kill those who were injured for food, and they would lift some out and keep them tied to a string and alive for a few days so their meat was fresh when they were killed, and some they would free to run away, when they had enough, because they never took more than the family could eat. Such greed would anger the gods and they would hold the rains back so the land became barren and everything turned to red dust. The rainbow snake would turn her face away from them, until the people withered and died.

He tracked around the edge of the forest, which now crackled fiercely as branches fell and the flames and smoke climbed higher. The distinctive smell of the trees pervaded the air for miles around, the same smell as when they boiled the sap to cure the brown leg sickness when you ate bad meat and your body could not keep its shit inside, and men would spend days away from the campfire. He also knew the leaves could be pounded into a paste with cold water and wiped onto cuts and wounds, to stop them bringing on the sweating death that sometimes followed an injury.

The people knew that even if it seemed they had killed the forest with their fire, in time the trees would grow new green branches, starting as a single leaf emerging from the charred black bark, and in a year or two the forest would be to all the world as if nothing had ever happened, and the inhabitants of the forest would return and make their homes there again, until the people came back this way and burnt it once more. So it had been for more time than anyone could remember.

When he reached the other side, he saw that the hunters

were busy, as he had known they would be. And around the
edges of the fire the women used wet branches to stop it
spreading to the grasslands, slashing at the fire as it reached
them to smother it and put it out, and stamping on loose
cinders. When the branches would themselves catch light,
they would throw them into the forest and the children
would bring them new branches from the pile they had
made earlier, and in this fashion they kept the fire contained
to where it was now. There was no wind, so no fiery embers
carried far. While they worked, some of the women sang,
excited at the prospect of food for all.

When the hunt was complete, they had killed three *nguyi*,
one so large it took two men to carry it. They had six dead
garril, too, and after giving respect to the spirits of all the
animals killed they immediately set to work taking the best
of the meat from the *garril* haunches, and lopping off their
tails, where the sweetest meat was. They wrapped the meat
in leaves, and later they would heat water in the family's one
large metal bowl—secured from traders a generation
before—and boil the tails for soup. The soup would be rich
and strong, the meat falling off the bones, and it would build
the children up after the time of walking that had brought
them here. There was one live *garril*, too, which whined on
the end of the bark-string to which it was tied.

It was a fair catch, and would let them build humpies by
the river, and they would all eat well for some time. He saw
his woman standing a little way off, her belly huge and her
hands behind her to support the weight, and smiled at her.
If all went well, it would be his first child, and born in a good
place.

When the food was all gathered, he looked to the old
man, sat under the shade of a large rock, and indicated the
way they should walk with a question in his eyes, and the
old man waved his hand in agreement. So he called to them
all, and they set off to find the waters. The family chattered
contentedly. He had done well, and with luck by nightfall
they would be gathering branches and grass to make the

humpies, and fresh food would be cooking.

The family's progress was closely watched by three men who had arrived on horseback, now lying on their bellies behind a high ridge to the West. Behind them, at the base of the ridge, were maybe a dozen more stockmen. Some were from the Gin Gin station, near Bundaberg, on the coast. And it was at Gin Gin that two men—brothers—had been speared to death by Aborigines apparently intent on stealing sheep.

The older of the men shaded his eyes, waving away flies with his hat.

"There's just too many of those black bastards for my liking. Look at them all."

His colleagues quietly nodded their agreement. "Look at that timber that's lost now," he murmured to them, indicating the smoking ruin of the forest. "We could have used that. And when they come round again," he indicated the land behind him with a sweep of his arm, "we'll have sheep all through here. I don't reckon they'll be eating wallaby then, right?"

He looked at them in grim determination. "So we all agreed?"

They were agreed. The men walked their horses back down the rise to the others.

By the river, as the new humpies were being erected, he banged two flintstones together and the sparks lit a small pile of grass and bark shavings, and within a few minutes a healthy fire was set. One of the youngest children jumped up and down in excitement, and he made a joke with her, telling her she looked like a baby *garril*.

The gunfire, when it started, came from where they had just been.

In abject terror, he saw one of the mothers clutch at

herself and fall, dropping the young child she was carrying, blood erupting from her chest.

Turning, he saw the men walking towards them, and in the same instant he saw their horses tied further away, and the long guns firing at his family repeatedly. He cursed, his eyes wild with anger and shock. He had been so pleased with the hunt, and the chance to settle for a few days, but he had not kept his eyes open for danger, though he was three days walk from where the white men lived and he had no idea why they would be here.

There was no time to think. The firing continued mercilessly. One by one, he saw his family fall, the red of their blood contrasting vividly with their dark skin. The old man threw a rock weakly towards the white men before being hit. He saw his mother's head explode into fragments.

He ran, panicked, to where the spears stood in the ground, but as his hands clutched at one of them his back was torn apart by at least three bullets and he died instantly.

When it was over, perhaps fifty lay dead. Perhaps more. The rider told one of the young men to use his machete and take the head of the black who lay by the spears. "We'll stick it on a pole to warn them off…stick it by the big gate."

One who had been with him on the ridge spoke quietly. "Mate, we'll need to tell the Governor, sometime. Make sure we're on the right side of the law."

"Yeah, but no hurry," he replied. "We had reason. We'll tell them one day when this mob are forgotten." He paused, scratching his chin, then turned to leave.

By the edge of the water, a young woman, her hands clutching at her bleeding and distended belly, was finished off with a pistol shot to the head.

As they walked back to the horses, they didn't even look round.

"No hurry. No one cares. Soon enough, eh? When we reach the city."

"The Hunt"

STEPHEN "YOLLY" YOLLAND is a writer and company director in Victoria, Australia. He has an enduring love of language, a strong social bent, and a tragic addiction to the Southampton Football Club—tragic since they play on the other side of the world. He was recently a finalist for the Ada Cambridge Biographical Prose Prize of 2019, and has a published volume of poetry called *Read Me*.

He says: "I was instantly intrigued by the idea and discipline of literary taxidermy, and for any Australian, *burn* always means *the bush*. On the driest continent on the planet, bushfire is integral to our life. From there, the opportunity to contrast two utterly different cultures, as well as reflect a real, historic incident, was simply too tempting to resist."

Goh Yong Ming Calvin

Yesterday

IT WAS A PLEASURE TO BURN after all these years. To fire up the system, to see the progress bar inching towards 100%. A simple, brainless procedure, but it brought back many memories.

There had been a considerable decline in business, and Jay's services tended towards desuetude. Nowadays everyone could do it themselves, with all the tools available commercially. Not that they were even relevant anymore. Burning had gone out of fashion, replaced by the almighty Cloud storage that boasted unrivalled convenience and accessibility—and free-of-charge. CDs and thumb drives were all rendered useless, a mere token that marked the swift demise of dated technology. The store was on its last leg, visited mostly by vagrants seeking shelter from the rain, or the occasional youth undergoing his gang's initiation rites. Sometimes, Jay played along, leaving out a case of 2GB thumb drives in the store camera's only blind-spot. They were pretty much worthless, so why not let the kids gain some street cred?

Jay had a soft spot for children. Over a decade ago, his wife had up and left, taking their kid with her, leaving behind nothing but a CD. On the disc was a single digital photo of the three of them: his visibly disgruntled wife cradling baby Oscar while he proudly cradled his own baby, a limited-edition gaming console complete with customisable parts. The attached .txt file was corrupted; Sophie never had affinity with technology. That summed up their whole relationship—they were never on the same page (or screen), and communications were ironically lost in the sea of applications that promised convenience. Jay set the photo as his desktop's wallpaper as a constant reminder of his folly, the moment before everything crumbled.

The divorce had hit hard, leaving Jay stuck in a rut. For the two years after he settled the proceedings, his store had remained closed, a shrine containing all the trinkets that ruined his life. During the hiatus, a government press release was issued, seeking to recall all optical and magnetic drives because of some inexplicable defect, but Jay, still deep in grief, chose to ignore it. Finally, in a valiant attempt to get back on his feet, he unironically opened for business, but found himself lagging far behind the present trends. The first day of his re-opening, customers stopped by and huddled in groups, murmuring and pointing at his outdated products and services. Jay pretended not to notice, but deep down he knew that his days were numbered. While he had sat about feeling sorry, technology—the one thing he had prided himself on knowing—had moved on with nary a backward glance. Now he knew how his wife had felt while she was with him. The store was a prime exhibit of the days before commercialized online storage and Jay was its faithful curator.

Rousing himself from his reverie, Jay sneaked a peek at the customer who made the request: a middle-aged man in a trench coat accompanied by a teenager glued to his tablet. The man had asked to burn a dozen copies of The Beatles' hit song "Yesterday" onto CDs as a party favour, of which the theme was, appropriately, Yesteryears. An easy but time-consuming task which left plenty of time for small talk.

"Haven't seen you 'round these parts before, where you from?"

"The city, but it's almost impossible to find anything there for a 90s throwback party, so I thought I'd try my luck out here." Behind the man, the teen exhaled an audible puff of air.

"Adam, can you keep yourself out of trouble for ten minutes while I conduct my business?" Adam rolled his eyes and skulked off to the aisles. Turning back to Jay, the man apologized.

"Sorry, kids these days, growing up alongside technology, they don't appreciate how good they've got things."

"Don't worry, it's probably just a phase. God knows I've been there." Jay peered over at Adam, who paced about the store, stopping to observe the occasional product with unconcealed disdain. Jay pegged him to be about Oscar's age. He tried to recall if he had ever been that scowly. Possibly when his father's affection for beepers denied him his first mobile phone. It's true then, what goes around comes around.

"I guess you're right." The man agreed before redirecting the conversation. "Quaint establishment you have here. To be quite honest, I wasn't expecting to find anyone who still did this. I thought all optical drives had been mass-recalled a couple of years back."

"Really? I must've missed that notice. Took a break for a couple years," Jay replied.

"I'm surprised you're still in business. But definitely not complaining." The man grinned.

"Not for long." Jay forced a chuckle. "But yeah, I'm holding on. Who knows? There may be more nostalgia parties looming over the horizon, and that's when I can make a comeback."

"Mm." The man mused. A pregnant pause hung in the air. Jay turned to check the status on the computer. The bar was paused at 75%. He issued a few commands which were promptly rejected.

"Damn thing's stuck again. Sorry for the delay."

"No worries. I remember the waiting; come to think of it, it wasn't so bad, I used to finish up chores while the files were transferring. 'Twas a simpler time indeed," the man replied as he rifled nonchalantly through the accessories on display.

"You got that right. If you ask me, today's technology, that's what's killing humanity," Jay ventured as he hurriedly relaunched the program. The bar reset to zero.

"How do you mean?"

"You know, with all the emphasis on convenience and accessibility nowadays, nobody actually spends time off their gadgets. Take it from me, I used to be one of the tech junkies, always keeping up to date on new releases to the point that my wife couldn't take it. She took my kid and left. I was broken, and by the time I picked myself up, it was too late. Ironic, isn't it, in a couple of years I went from tech tycoon to a living fossil in the business." Jay sighed. "I'd be lying if I said I had no regrets." His eyes trailed to his desktop wallpaper, just as Adam returned from the back aisles.

"There's some truth to that," the man conceded. "Really makes you wonder, doesn't it? With digital closeness usurping the physical, are human connections even possible anymore? Or have we been unwittingly enslaved by technology?" The computer chose this moment to erupt in a series of beeps.

"Damnit. I'm sorry, there must be something wrong with the function—"

"I can help." Without asking for permission, Adam spun the keyboard over and tapped the keys with a graceful flourish. Jay watched with fascination as the computer gave a satisfied chime and the bar shot to completion. The kid folded his arms, smirking.

"Show-off," the man muttered. Jay bagged the CDs and handed them over. "Time to go. Nice meeting you." He nodded at Jay before walking out.

Adam loitered, waiting for the man to leave. Then he leaned towards Jay and whispered, "Out with the old, in with the new." Grinning, he exited. As if on cue, Jay's computer force-started, playing The Beatles' "Yesterday." Jay could only watch helplessly as the melancholic chords and McCartney's voice cut off, to be replaced by the dreaded BSOD—the Blue Screen of Death.

Outside, the sky was overcast. Bundling themselves into the car, the man revved the engine.

"Did you get it done?"

"Of course, I'm a professional," Adam retorted.

"So what happens next?" The man looked up at the sky. The clouds had parted, giving way to a light drizzle. Adam swiped a few strokes on his tablet.

"The virus is queued to run after the second verse. When it's done, nothing can salvage that heap of junk. Actually, even without me it would've probably expired in the next year or two."

"You know what the boss said. We have to purge all existing personal storage before we can proceed to the next phase."

"Yeah, yeah, planned obsolescence and all that. I was at the briefing too, y'know. Where to next?"

"Well, for now, just sit tight. They'll give us our next assignment when we reach the city."

"Yesterday"

GOH YONG MING CALVIN is a student in Singapore. He is a huge fan of American sitcoms, in particular *Brooklyn Nine-Nine*, *The Office*, and *Friends*, all of which he has re-watched many times from start to end. He sings in a choir (fifteen years and counting!) and loves creative writing—although without a deadline, procrastination usually triumphs. But not this time! "Yesterday" is his first submission to a writing competition and his first published short story.

He says: "My undergraduate thesis required me to submit a physical CD containing a PDF copy of my research paper—and it took me a few days to find both a rewritable disc and a working CD-reader. By chance this was exactly when I learned of this year's Literary Taxidermy competition, and the inspiration for this story came to me as I watched the copying-in-progress status bar inch its way across the screen. I distinctly remember feeling a touch of nostalgia beneath the frustration of dealing with outdated technology; and the story pretty much wrote itself after that."

In Defense of an Innocent

IT WAS A PLEASURE TO BURN. To bleed. To be consumed. To give up one's flesh for one's master—nothing else in the world as we know it could simulate the ecstasy of such sacrifice.

To understand this essential truth is the key to understanding Ralph Pettingroom, and his decision at the fresh age of twenty-three to surrender his life and body to the consumption of someone else.

Actually, Ralph's obsession with being eaten had started much earlier, as these things tend to—in his childhood.

We often hear it said that children cannot make memories before the age of about three, but Ralph did. His earliest memory, from two-and-a-half years old, involved an incident of his mother sucking on his little white infant calf. Ralph had been bitten by a brown recluse as he lay naked upon a blanket in the yard of his family's property in Illinois, but Ralph didn't remember that detail. What he did remember was the image of his mother's teeth, long and white with pointed incisors, pressed into his fragile baby leg, as she tried to suck the poison out of the wound.

In this memory, little Ralph hadn't been able to understand what his mother was doing, and in his underdeveloped baby brain he had thought she was eating him.

But instead of feeling fearful, Ralph in his helpless and vulnerable state found himself feeling quite surrendered, quite free, caressed within the jaw of his trusted mother, whom he loved dearly with all his heart. In fact, in the version Ralph remembered, a tiny infant boner sprouted up between his legs which made his mother gasp, recoiling from him.

From there the fixation only blossomed.

At the age of five, little Ralphie enrolled in school. Being a resident in a small rural community meant that children in school were not granted the relief of anonymity among their peers. Not only did every kid know every other kid, but every other kid knew every other kid's mom, and those moms knew the dads, and the dads knew the grandmoms, and so on, back and back and back. In this way, early reputations were hard to outgrow.

Within the first week of school, Ralphie's fate was sealed for the next thirteen years of his life. He became thereafter referred to as *deerboy*.

The younger children at the school liked to play a game of chase in which a group of boys would chase girls around the playground. These boys called themselves wolves and would howl in unison to signal their attack. In turn, the girls, or prey, would screech and scatter into different directions, pouting and promptly limping in defeat to the yard supervisor in the rare case they were ensnared by one of the boys.

Ralphie, however, went against the implicit rules of the game. Refusing to play as a wolf, he ran among the girls as they fled, screaming in a high pitched voice as confused wolves avoided him, choosing other targets. When finally one boy did acknowledge him, Ralphie bellied-up square in the center of the playground, making no attempt to evade the impending attack. Whimpering and writhing under the striking fists of his classmate, Ralphie didn't let up until a teacher pulled the two of them apart. Opening his eyes, he asked to the other boy, "Why'd you stop?"

School age was hard on Ralphie. As he grew into a stout and chubby little blue-eyed boy, he struggled finding friends who understood him. The other children were quite fond of drawing antlers on his tests and papers when they were passed forward to be turned in, or grabbing him by the neck and pushing his face into trashcans between classes. Kid stuff. And yet, we've all heard it said—when a door closes, a window opens. Ralphie found his window through anime.

Every day after school, Ralphie used to come home, throw off his school bag, and scuttle into the family office, ignoring the requests of his mother to bring down used dishes out of his room. He would boot up the 1990's-era Windows computer the family shared, staring into the age-tinted white box as the checkered logo loaded on the screen.

For hours, Ralphie would watch any anime he could gain access to, clicking the home button whenever he heard the office door rattle behind him. His parents' curiosity satisfied as he scrolled the articles of Yahoo news, he would click the back button at their departure, continuing to absorb precious hours of *hentai* and *yaoi*.

It was only a matter of time before he discovered his second love DeviantArt.

Now a budding teenager, Ralph decided to try his hand as an artist, depicting truths which he felt were lacking in the online art community. His primary interest, of course was vore.

In the beginning of his art career, Ralph preferred to use crayons. He still owned a pack of over one hundred colors he'd gotten at his tenth birthday party, and it was the most logical medium at the time. However, Ralph's childhood home didn't have a scanner, and his initial uploads of sideways, uncropped captures from his flip phone received waves of negative feedback and accusations of potato photography from the community he so cherished. As a result, Ralph transitioned into the controversial medium of MS Paint.

Before we put ourselves in the position to critique an artist's work, we must consider his circumstances.

Truly, Ralph was no Picasso. But perhaps he was a Van Gogh—representing a style misunderstood by his peers.

His favorite subject to depict was himself. Himself, being devoured by the beloved characters of his most adored anime series. Reclining in the fattened and transparent stomach of his favorite Japanese vulpine character. Engulfed to the torso by the mouth of an oversized *waifu* as the city of Tokyo lay smashed under her high-heeled sole.

If it hasn't been made clear, Ralph also loved crushing and macro.

Once he had reached the legal age to do so, Ralph joined online dating sites. Finding himself too bashful to message the guys, he focused on the girls, who more often smiled in their pictures, accepting him with their easy eyes. He had a list of templates saved on a private document, which he would of course personalize before sending:

what would u do if I was tiny at ur bare feet ?

vampires or foxes ;] :D ?

if I was a chair would u break me ?

Though he never got a response, Ralph found his own joy in sending the messages. Sometimes, even seeing the green dot signaling a girl's online status was enough to rile him into a passionate jerking session, his eyes toggling between the inanimate expression of the girl's default thumbnail and his message which he imagined her reading. He would fantasize catching her, pinning her, in the unconscious tangent of her brain that had processed his words. A forbidden love.

Luckily for Ralph, there were other outlets for his insatiable desires besides the unappreciative online consumers of his art and poetry. He found solace in the plight of those cinematic fictional characters whose misunderstood needs were familiar to his own.

Anthony Hopkins as Hannibal Lecter was his first celebrity crush with Gaspard Ulliel a close second.

On his eighteenth birthday, after breakfast at his favorite pancake diner with his family, Ralph had hurried upstairs, closing himself in his room and pushing his TV-recorded tape of *Hannibal Rising* into the old VCR, having a full blown marathon for the entirety of the two hour runtime. The next morning he couldn't hold a pencil steady without his hand cramping, and his mother yelled at him to stop drinking soda in the bedroom as his sheets were sticking together in the laundry.

Though he was no Casanova, Ralph wasn't a total novice in the realm of tangible sexual encounters. That is to say, he had a grand total of two substantial confrontations he counted towards his experience.

The first was at the age of nine, during summer camp. He and another boy peed in the woods together, offering some justification to hold each other's undergrown wieners for aim. Another group of kids had surprised them from behind, and as an automatic reflex the second boy had started beating the breath out of an exposed and unsuspecting Ralphie, which only made the experience more erotic and memorable.

The second happened when Ralph was nineteen, blue-haired, rosy-cheeked and soft around the edges, ears pierced with black gauges that looked like melanoma against his pale skin. It was bedbound, vanilla sex between him and the brother of his community-college roommate, on the last day of an anime convention. Ralph came prematurely and cried afterward, covering his face with the powder-blue comforter they were wrapped in.

If it hasn't been made clear, Ralph hated his penis almost more than he hated himself.

The shape of Ralph's member was a microcosm of Ralph's overall body shape. And the way it performed under pressure was a microcosm of Ralph.

His penis was just shy of four inches long, with a wide girth that bulged around the center. Uncircumcised, the head only peeked out halfway when erect, causing a ring of discoloration to imprint along the edge of the glans from years of built-up precum sodium deposits.

Now, we as abject viewers could look at such a thing and recognize the beauty in it, the uniqueness. Nature's tattoo. A swirling constellation of pearly papules.

Ralph, however, was unable to see beyond the stamp of deformity. In his artistic musings, he rejected his appendage, often drawing himself with deliberate anatomical inaccuracy, or as a eunuch altogether.

A suicidal college dropout with no close friends, no serious aspirations, and no career prospects, Ralph Pettingroom found his salvation at the age of twenty-two. It came in the form of an old news story shared online. The headline read:

German Man Consents to Cannibalism By Lover, Overcooks Penis

Here it was that Ralph came to learn the story of Bernd Jurgen Armando Brandes, an engineer from Berlin who'd responded to a posting on a secret forum for cannibals, now defunct. Apparently, Brandes had agreed to be slaughtered and eaten by the stranger who'd made the posting. Upon the pair's sanctified meeting, Brandes had suggested the added pleasure of having his penis amputated as a delicacy for the two of them to share, but a cooking mishap had caused most of his meat to go to the dog instead.

For Ralph, finding out there were others in the real world with goals aligned to his was like a test-monkey being released into the wild, among its native species for the first time.

Without wasting another moment, Ralph fashioned his own posting. His next move was to publish the finished product on every forum of which he was an active user, which included Reddit, Craigslist, Anime.com and eBay. His accounts on each of the aforementioned sites were immediately banned. The ingenuous entreaty had been written as such (edited for spelling):

> M4A ISO master dom to consume my naked flesh. cooked or raw. man/woman ok. big women preferred. fat ok. animal morph ok.

Despite the initial negative response, Ralph was persistent. Eventually he caught on to the darkweb as a more appropriate intermediary for his appeal, refreshing his posting every few weeks once it became buried among other user requests.

It took almost a year—eight months and twenty-seven days, to be exact—for someone to answer. But the response Ralph finally received was worth the wait. It read:

> Hello there, my name is Theodore. My friends call me Dore. You can call me Theo if it's easier. I saw your posting and am deeply interested. I'm located on the East coast but I own a truck so driving isn't a problem. I hope you don't mind me asking, but how much do you weigh? I have some mason jars in my basement I could use to store your organs on my drive back, but if your volume exceeds 300 liters, I'll have to go and buy more. Look forward to hearing from you,

-Dore-

Ralph was elated. In his follow-up, he poured out his heart, his history, his whole world in a way he'd never done before.

Satisfied with the correspondence, Ralph solidified arrangements, deciding it would be best to do the deed on a weekend when his parents were out of town, so he would have the house to himself.

We can't underestimate the range of emotions Ralph would have been feeling when that fateful night finally arrived.

All his life had led him to this moment—the moment he had dreamed about for months, and pined after for years without knowing it.

Ralph was a gracious host. That night he had adapted a forced seductive quality to his voice. Nervous as he surely must have been, Ralph was careful to disguise the excited trembling in his elbows and knees, sitting ever calmly, not before pulling out the chair across from him with grace and efficacy. A gentleman.

"There's a bottle of white Chardonnay, some seasonings, and a ready injection of morphine on the table by the frying pan," he said in a husky drawl, his blue eyes twinkling over candles he'd placed along the table. "I'd love to watch you eat my cock."

He swiftly added, "Sear it on a low heat. With the pan cover is probably best. It's a kind of thick so the outside might burn otherwise." He had been watching reruns of chef competition shows for weeks leading up to that night.

The amputation was seamless. Ralph suffered no pain. He didn't so much as squeak.

It wasn't until we stood over the sizzling pan, his plump sex organ shrinking and hissing over its pool of bloodied chardonnay, that Ralph burst into tears.

I did my best to comfort him through the remainder of the process, hushing his coos as I helped him wash down the rest of the Xanax. Drugs can have such effects though, making a person overly doubtful of every decision. I assured him that everything would be okay, even cradled him for a bit before his body went limp. I didn't mind that the first course would be cold by the time I returned to it.

Ralph will always be very special to me, as it was both of our first times. One thing I didn't expect was how hot a person could be on the inside. As I look out at the rows of trees and cornfields which border the highway, I wonder, musingly, if a deer's organs are as radiating as a human's. I turn Ralph's plastic-wrapped view so that he can look too.

We'll need to find a cooler soon. When we reach the city.

"In Defense of an Innocent"

SHEL MERLOW is an interviewer, teacher, and editor living in the Czech Republic. She always had a talent for making people uncomfortable and decided at an early age to channel that into her writing. "In Defense of an Innocent" is her first published short story.

She says: "A friend was telling me the story about the incident with the German man and his lover that appears in my story, and I was just thinking how weird it must be to become infamous for such a fetish. People always want to look back on a person's life to understand what influences led to a certain outcome, and I was playing into that a bit for this story."

Ronnie

IT WAS A PLEASURE TO BURN. That's what my husband Brian said. He fed the contents of Veronica Hadley-Cross' suitcase, her leather Louis Vuitton handbag, Gucci trousers, Chanel shirts, and Jimmy Choo stilettos one-by-one into the barrel burner in the back garden a year after she had first appeared, a year minus four days after she had died. He thought he'd burnt everything—but he was wrong.

"I want a double room. Tomorrow. For the week." Her voice rumbled down the phone late Saturday night, too posh for our prices, too southern for our part of the country and I swear to God she sounded like my girlhood idol, Kathleen Turner. Smoky, sexy, thrilling as distant thunder. I should have taken note. A storm was heading my way.

"Is it ensuite?" she asked.

"You're in luck. I have only one ensuite, it was taken but the party cancelled this morning," I said, relieved that the room would not lie fallow in this busy, high income week.

"How much?"

Late booking, single-occupancy, high-demand because of the new gallery opening. Ding, dong. I gave her the high season tariff bumped twenty percent.

"With full English—"

"No breakfast."

"The room's one-fifty a night."

"And what do I get for that? Gold taps and sea views?"

"Partial." I ignored the taps crack. "Partial sea view." No need to mention she would have to stand on the balcony, lean out and squint down the hill between the five-story hotel-converted townhouses and hope the mist hadn't rolled in off the North Sea. No. No need.

"Sea views are over-bloody-rated," she said. "And I want to smoke."

"This is a no smoking establishment."

"I'll pay extra."

Someone who was used to calling the shots then.

"One hundred and fifty pounds to steam clean when you vacate the room. And a late booking fee." Purely arbitrary on my part, but I was beginning to not like her tone.

She agreed. Not that she had much choice. August, the town was booked to the gills, more than was usual because of the high-profile (as the weekly paper labelled it) inaugural exhibition at *Northern Waves* including names whose work usually evoked wows, unspoken bewilderment and prices beyond reasonable doubt. A misguided, in my view, project to bring more culture to the northeast by the Lord Darlington Estate and the Tate Modern but who was I to complain when it meant increased custom? *It's always good to count blessings,* Mam would say, *but counting pennies makes more sense.* Mam, God rest her soul, had a point. Always. About every-bloody-thing.

"So, that's confirmed?"

I thought twice about taking her reservation. Wondered if she was not English. Not a problem. I've had some very nice foreign guests. Often more polite than many of our home-grown guests in my opinion. Mam always said *the Empire took manners as well as trade to the colonies.* But I decided her buried vowels were a result of a private education boarding school not a mission school and I folded away my doubts. *A let was a let was dinner on the table,* as Mam would say. And a thousand quid plus extras was doing a rah-rah with pompoms in my brain.

I took her name—Veronica Hadley-Cross, a mouthful and definitely not working class—and she rattled off her credit card details which meant she had it ready or the numbers were etched on the inside of her eyelids. Visa Platinum, if you please. Paid in full. Either the Metropole and Royal were booked out or had refused her smoking diktat.

In my profession, you learn to read people. Clearly, she was connected to the showing. She sounded the type. Opinionated. Bossy. Curator or critic on an expense account, creaming a few pennies off an over-generous allowance, even with my extras. I've had plenty of those sorts staying at Seaview Heights (I thought the *Heights* helped offset any trade description objections); journos, regional salesmen and salesladies—yes we know feminism and equality—conference organisers and of course the usual assortment of B, C, or D-list celebrities, soap stars and game show hosts—all what Mam called *leftover sirloin roast reduced to hotpot.* And in my not inconsiderable experience, even the well-heeled and well-connected can't resist making money when they have the chance.

Give me and Maria, my eagle-eyed housekeeper, a day or two, and Mrs Veronica Hadley-Cross would slip into the right slot. Not that I was really interested. The who or what or why didn't matter to me. It is a matter of pride that I never, never pry into the personal circumstances of my guests, nor do I indulge in idle speculation. Not my place. Mam's mantra and she drilled it into all of us was *mind yours, and never mind theirs.*

Next time, I'll follow my bloody instincts.

On Sunday afternoon—afternoon mind—Davy Jones' cab pulled up. No not *the* Davy Jones. He died years ago. Our Davy Jones was a Swansea fugitive who'd married a local lass, although he often cadged free pints down the King's Head belting out *Daydream Believer* until he grew fat and his baby-face got too craggy.

Veronica Hadley-Cross fell out of the taxi, pissed as the proverbial newt. Her black leather stilettos with bondage buckles designed to tumble catwalk models, did their job. Halfway up the steps to the front door, she stumbled, recovered and limped on. Davy dumped her small suitcase and cabin bag in the hallway.

"Pay the man and put it on my bill," she said from behind her over-sized Anna Wintour sunglasses despite the overcast day, rubbing her right ankle, oblivious to her ripped tights and her left knee peppered with blood. A coat, more op shop than vintage, of rabbit fur, sick rabbit not mink, swamped her sparrow-like frame.

"You've got a right one here, my lovely," Davy whispered in my ear. I handed him a tenner. "Gavin at the station said she fell off the train. Blotto apparently. I'll keep the change, I've earned it."

"Mrs Hadley-Cross, welcome."

"Mzzz Hadley-Cross. My friends call me Ronnie." Her words and hands oozed like sludge.

"Ronnie then."

"I said friends. You're not there yet."

I most certainly did not care to be her friend because while I'd never been scared of a guest, Veronica Hadley-Cross made every instinct clang as if Quasimodo himself was ringing bells upstairs in the partial sea-view family room. But Davy had driven off, she'd paid handsomely and this was business. *Friends cost money, guests pay money. Don't confuse the two, Jean.* Another of Mam's lessons learnt after a lifetime in the hospitality business.

Up close, her pinned hair, more nicotine than blonde, clumped in thick rat nests as if unbrushed for years. Think Trump on a bad hair day. Yes, difficult I know. Mzzz Veronica Hadley-Cross, her face camouflaged baldly by shouty makeup (what Mam would call cheap showgirl), was at best sixty at worst seventy.

I showed her to the room, thanking what Mam called *the God of Small Mercies* that her room was up the steep Victorian stairs, away from other guests.

"The dining room opens for breakfast at six-thirty—" she snorted "—until ten o'clock. No exceptions. We have a terrace, if the weather's nice."

She took a deep breath, held it and looked around, her carmine lips pursed, nose wrinkled.

"Terrace? I think not. Besides, I told you I didn't want breakfast. And you forgot my ashtray. Or will the floor do?"

Her tobacco-coloured fingers scrabbled in her vintage Louis Vuitton handbag. She dug out an enamelled and gilt cigarette case. Deeper excavation and more muttered profanities produced not a lighter but one of those long-nosed candle-lighting gizmos you buy in Poundland. Her painted dragon-fire fingertips, flickering like bonfire sparks, inched out a cigarette, which she slotted between her puckered lips. With the exaggerated deliberation of a drunk, she fired up the lighter-wand and leaned into it. The cigarette trembled in its flame. She inhaled. Once. Twice. Eyes closed, the look on her face was that of a woman ebbing after orgasm. The same look I imagined on mine, eyes also closed, when in the dark, after my Brian has done his business but not mine, after he has rolled over and started snoring, after I have quietly done what he couldn't do. That look.

She lay wrapped in her coat, shoes kicked on the floor like tired kittens, still wearing her Gucci sunglasses when I brought her a pot of coffee with the ashtray.

She waved a vein-corded hand at me. "Take that crap away. Never drink it after midday."

"Have you had a long journey, Ms Hadley-Cross?"

"Fucking trains, had to change twice. I told you, it's Ronnie."

Clearly, I'd made the leap.

"What brings you so far up north?" She ignored me.

Well, I wasn't used to that. "Any special plans? The exhibition? The spa? The coastal trail?"

She lifted her glasses and gave me a salty stare.

"Do I look like I walk fucking coastal paths?" Her laughter was not encouraging.

"Right. Just so you are aware, I lock the hotel at ten p.m. If you need anything urgently out of hours, my cell number is in the information leaflet."

"Then I'll need a fucking key."

During breakfast next morning, there were complaints of a herby, no spicy, no a bit of both, smell coming from Ronnie's room overnight. And singing. And, shock, horror, laughter. And other unspecified unseemly noises. After midnight.

Probably the television on too loud, I told them. She's in her sixties. I hoped to God it was the television but a wee part of me smiled behind my tuts. However, my guests, good people, boring people, were regulars so I went to have a word with her, but she'd slipped out and by the time I left that evening hadn't returned.

Later, Maria binned four empty wine bottles, a mini Everest of dead cigarettes, a still warm cannabis squib, half-eaten pizza, two scorched pillowslips and a cushion stained and drenched with Australian Merlot from her room.

I left a note, informing her of fire hazards, costs incurred and requesting she keep *the television volume down!*

Tuesday morning, a young man in spray-on leathers, carrying a crash helmet and an insulated delivery bag stood at the breakfast room door.

"You might want to check on Ronnie," he said. "She's space walking. Dunno what we took, but Jesus, for an oldie…shit. If I lose this job, it'll have been worth it." He headed for the front door, *PIZZA PRONTO* emblazoned in red, white and green across his back.

Ronnie lay naked on the bed, singing *He Did It My Way à la* Sinatra. She sat up when I entered. No modesty. No shame.

"Bring me coffee. Hot and strong like that young man who just left." She laughed like an unblocked drain and wiped what I briefly mistook for blood then hoped was pizza sauce smeared over her bare breasts.

I returned with coffee as she came out of the bathroom wearing only red polka dot bikini briefs, the sort fifteen-year olds buy from *Primark*. The sort I'd longed for as a girl. Her breasts hung pendulous and her belly puckered from age and an old scar. Upright, her thighs without the benefit of nylon were dimpled and veined like a ripe Stilton. War paint on, hair pinned, she stood, legs apart, right hand slouched on her hip as she poured the coffee. She didn't give a damn and, in that moment, I loved her.

"Ms Hadley-Cross, I run a respectable house here. I must ask you to leave." I worked those words hard to sound like I meant them. What I wanted to say was you go girl. And maybe, take me with you.

Teeth clenched to stop her cigarette from falling, her smoke-filled eyes squinty, she said, "I've paid for my room."

Sultry. Glamorous. Dangerous. My Kathleen Turner in *Body Heat*. I was excited just looking at her.

After an hour ringing around, I found her a room at Margery Connolly's Old Custom House Hotel near the port. I told Margery Ronnie wanted something nearer the sea, closer to the centre. I lied that the hill to mine was difficult for an older lady. Margery had a couple of guests, women she was convinced were in an unholy alliance. I offered to take them in exchange, at a reduced rate. That swung the deal.

After two more hours of Ronnie's verbal abuse, full reimbursement of the paid week, the extra hundred pounds late booking fee and another hundred on top *for her inconvenience,* I finally got her out of the house. Maria did a rush job cleaning and fumigating the room. Clare and Jennifer were delighted, not just with the partial sea view and cheaper rate, including full English, but to be away from the disapproving lifts of Margery's Pentecostal eyebrows.

The sirens woke me and the town just after midnight. By morning, nothing was left of Margery Connolly's Old Custom House, but ashes and wisps of smoke released by the last embers sizzling in the rain.

I took no part in the speculation or blame afterwards but did offer to take Ronnie's suitcase which had somehow survived the flames for safekeeping until kith or kin claimed them. No one ever did.

The nights Brian went down the pub, I'd put on those red knickers, tell Mam to keep her thoughts to herself and swan around the house in Ronnie's coat and fuck-me Louboutin shoes.

At night, she'd come to me. She'd sit on the end of my bed, look at Brian snoring, look at me, cross her legs and light up.

"Are you really planning to die like this? With him? With this life?"

"And where would I go, Ronnie? What would I do? This," I looked at Brian's back, "this is all I know."

"Bollocks. You have money—I know how much you've got tucked away in the accounts. The accounts he doesn't know about. You've thought about doing a runner since forever. You just need me, don't you girl?"

"I'm not a girl."

"No, but did I ever let that stop me? I bloody well had fun up to the moment I died. Watching those flames lick up Margery fucking Connolly's jacquard curtains was beautiful. It was a pleasure to watch them burn. And what you shall do, I don't know yet. But I tell you, we will know. When we reach the city."

"Ronnie"

SHANNON SAVVAS is a New Zealand writer who divides her heart and life between Cyprus, England, and New Zealand. She takes photographs of unnoticed things, particularly the small marvelous structures in nature, and the beauty of plants past their prime. She is a former-nurse, and has been published both online and in print. In addition to her success with literary taxidermy, she is the short-fiction winner of the 2019 Over the Edge New Writing Prize at the Cúirt Literary festival in Galway.

She says: "A newspaper article about a nightmare guest in a small hotel sparked this story, but it never felt right or complete until I considered fitting it into the 2019 Literary Taxidermy prompt. Doing so breathed life into the story, giving me a real sense of my narrator."

Sunshade, Starlight

IT WAS A PLEASURE TO BURN the giant paper fish. I never told Sun that. She was fond of it—she'd even named it, in the few short days she stole it from my father and went on the run. *Will it hurt Dayu, to burn him?* I told her no. The truth is, I didn't know, but I knew I wanted to burn the fish. It had the mark of my father's craft all over it. The merciless sharp folds, incantations inscribed in bold black ink, scars scored against its heaving belly.

But I didn't tell Sun, not because she was fond of the fish, but because I was ashamed at the twisted spark of joy I felt. The cold star-like gleam that flared up within me when we built the bonfire in the middle of the courtyard and gave the fish's broken body to the flames. Watching my father's handiwork go to ashes. Listening to that silky crunchy burning sound.

Looking back, there was something of a strange purification about that moment. As if, by burning this beast my father had made, I was burning away something inside me too, a part of him I had folded so impossibly small it was wedged like a splinter in my ribs.

The day Sun crashed into my temple, I was sweeping the leaves in the garden. One moment, I heard a cry from above and looked up to see a girl on the back of a fish, and the next she had plummeted from the sky and landed in a heap at my feet. She crawled out from under the wreck, looking like a wild spirit with twigs in her braid.

She was badly bruised—Sun, that is, not the fish. The fish was male. Not that it mattered much to either of them, because the fish was at death's door. It had a huge gash in one side of its belly, the breath had gone right out of it, and the orange markings had faded. It was a stunning feat of papercrafting, and I would have run as far away from it as I could if I had anywhere to go.

"Ouch," Sun muttered, and looked up at me. Her eyes widened. "You!"

I had already thrown down my rake and reached into my pocket for a piece of paper. I didn't like doing this, but I carried paper around only for times like these.

"Ugh, I'm sorry, I lost control of Dayu and—hey!"

With surprising swiftness, she turned on her ankle and spun out of the way of the paper star I'd sent flying at her. It lodged itself into the chestnut tree behind her instead.

"I wouldn't have killed you. I just wanted to pin you to the tree," I said.

"Do you always welcome your guests this way?"

"You're not a guest. You're an intruder. And a thief."

Sun's eyebrows shot up. She smiled. "A thief?"

I nodded at the fish, lying on the ground between us. The sun was setting. With the flames from all the lit braziers flaring up in the evening breeze, the fish seemed, almost, to be alive again, the shadows a burnished crimson orange dappled across its great body. But then a cloud passed, and the colour vanished.

"That's a royal mount," I said. "And you're no royal."

Sun turned and spat on the ground.

"Damn right I'm no royal. What're you gonna do about it? Report me?"

I said nothing. There was a smirk on Sun's face. "Didn't think so, Wen Ronglin."

I was already starting to back away from her, but now I froze. Sun crossed her arms. "You don't remember me, do you?"

She reached into her pack, pulled out a paper packet, and tossed it at me. I kept my eyes narrowed on her as I unwrapped it. Two rice cakes fell into my hands.

I stared at them, then up at her. Her smile was already fading.

"We need you. Come back to the city."

"I'm just Lin now," I said, and turned away.

We don't forget what we learn from our fathers, the good and the bad. I learned how to fold paper stars that shone with their own light, and she learned how to pound flour until her calluses had calluses.

I remembered her, a gangly girl too tall for her age, a few years older than I was. The daughter of the palace cook. She lived outside of the main compound, and I saw her sometimes from my window. She would run around the lotus pond with the other children, fall and scrape her knees, and get up again. Her hands and clothes were always floury.

She learned how to make the best rice cakes in the imperial city, and I learned how to smile through the pain of a thousand paper cuts.

The thing about trying to run away from paper was, I didn't have a lot of it, and the gash in the fish was huge. I spent one week turning the temple upside down for stacks of unused rice paper, parchment, even scrolls that had once held prayers and lines of poetry, long faded. I wasted so many sheets trying to figure out the folds and incantations my father had used, trying to patch up the fish as best as I could to get Sun out of here, fast.

Sun, meanwhile, was no help.

"When we reach the city—"

"I told you," I said, kneeling over the fish, working the seams of a devilish fold in its fin, "I'm not going."

"—I'm sure they'll know you right away. And then everything will be okay."

"What makes you think it'll be okay?"

"You're the only papercrafter in the land strong enough to take down the Chief Minister! The guards are on our side, Lin, you know they are. The whole city is."

I sat back on my heels, fists clenched tight on my lap. "He's not a god," I said.

Sun shrugged. "He thinks he is. He might as well be."

She was standing at the doorway, the wisteria blooming at her shoulder, sunset at her back. She looked like she had been here for years. There was a bowl of rice cakes on the kitchen counter that she had made this morning, a little mountain of them.

I was starting to shake. I had to stand up and take a deep breath, walk to the window and gaze out at the stone face of the mountain. How small I was, in its shadow. How the wind and snow would break, melt, become as nothing against its majestic peaks. No, my father was no god, and neither was I. I had come here to remember this. I had run away to remember this.

I tried to chalk it up to the lengthening days, the rising heat, the way Sun hummed as she stoked the fire on the stove and boiled soup from roots I never even knew were growing in my backyard, but in the end I had to admit: it was the fish. I wasn't hallucinating. The more time I spent with it, the more I heard his whip-burn voice in my head. *One more fold. Ten more. A hundred.* My skin stung when I touched his brushwork.

I told Sun, "It's like trying to paint into someone else's painting."

"Does that mean you can't do it?" Sun asked, kneeling down next to me.

I ran a hand gingerly over the fish. "The beast's wounds

are too severe. Look at its belly. Its fins. That nick on its tail. It was scarred long before you ever stole him. Aren't I right?"

Sun flew to her feet. "Dayu's not a *beast*."

I touched the gash again. It was serrated at the edges, the paper ripped in a harsh, ragged way. Sun had never said, and I'd never asked, but I knew the marks of an imperial arrow. "You were shot at, weren't you?"

"I was trying to save him," said Sun, biting the words off between her teeth. "I was trying to set him free. I didn't think they'd shoot him. His own mount! Chief Minister Wen is a monster."

I looked down at my hands. Without knowing it, I'd started folding another star with the closest piece of paper. They'd always come easiest to me. I used to fold them at night, looking up at the sky from the battlements, the guards tiny below me. So tiny, I could fold little paper men bigger than them. I was trying to save him too. Just that I didn't know it, back then. I thought I was trying to save myself, but the truth was, I was always trying to save my father.

"We need to burn it," I said. "I don't want a trace of my father's papercraft remaining in this house. And then we're going to the market to get all the paper we can find, and I'll make you a new mount."

"Us. You mean, make *us* a new mount," said Sun.

I shook my head. "I'm not going back with you."

Sun set her mouth in a thin line. Before I could say anything more, she turned and disappeared into the forest behind the shrine.

I didn't know what I was promising. Of course I could make a mount. I had folded and breathed life into hundreds of little paper flowers, horses, soldiers, for this moment. My father had said, *Ronglin, you'll be Chief Minister one day. You will be good.* It wasn't a prediction. It was an instruction. I knew that, and my hubris got the better of me anyway.

I had never made anything so big before. Day by day, I sat out in the courtyard, folding and joining paper, sweating till I grew pale and bled constantly from the cuts on my fingertips. The season was turning. Summer was at its height. The better for me, the more daylight to work by, but the hours were long, the heat leaving me dry as a bone in the desert.

Sun didn't speak to me for three days. She just kept making rice cakes. I think she made them for the same reason I fold stars. When she finally broke her silence, coming up to me one afternoon, she said, "That's not a fish."

"Fish are my father's emblem. He likes them…especially golden carp. I don't want to make a fish," I said.

Sun crouched down across from me and watched me work. "It looks like a bird."

"She." I patted the bird's neck, stroked it gently. The breath within was beginning to stir at last. "She's an eagle. I wanted to make you a mount that would feel…free."

Sun sat back, hugged her knees to her chest and fixed me with a searching gaze. "Is that why you won't come back? Because you don't feel free?"

I started to shake my head, then paused. In truth, I didn't know the answer. I'd thought I was free, here in the mountain, but I couldn't run forever.

Sun got up, went back into the house and returned with a plate for me. There was a fresh batch of rice cakes on it. I picked one up, took a bite and savoured the sweet bean paste in my mouth. Its simplicity rooted me where I sat. I didn't need to make it so complicated. I was making an amazing work right here and now, and I wasn't doing it for power or glory.

"I think there are still things I can do from here," I said.

It took me another forty days and nights to finish the eagle. Sun was next to me in the courtyard when I fixed the last feather into place. I laid my hands over the eyes on the eagle's great head, crowned in white, and I felt her sigh and shudder, and all the breath in my body whooshed out of me then flared up again, mighty and limitless.

"She's awake, isn't she," Sun whispered.

I nodded, and removed my hands. The eagle opened her eyes, reared her head as though waking from a long, long nap. Perhaps some part of her had been sleeping inside me all along.

"It's an honour to meet you," said Sun. She tiptoed and offered her hand. The eagle inclined its head, nestling it briefly in her palm.

"The wind is changing," I said. "You should go."

Sun looked at me, eyes wide. "Now?"

I nodded. "Now."

A sudden gust swept the dry earth, the ashes, up from the courtyard and down the mountain.

As Sun hitched her pack onto her shoulder and turned to face me, I thought she might ask me again to go with her. But she let out a sharp exhale, smiled, and leapt up onto the back of the eagle.

"Thank you," was all she said, and then she took off.

I stood in the courtyard and watched her go. The flames in the braziers flickered, seemed to grow brighter, then dimmer, in the shadow of the great eagle as it took to the wind. I watched until Sun had faded into the horizon and the clouds had swallowed her up.

"Thank you," I murmured in return.

Then I turned back and went into my room. I sat down on the floor, picked up a piece of paper, and began to fold a star, and another, and another after that.

Today, a boy from the village brought a letter from her. There's only one word on it: *Lin.* I turn it over, and on the other side is my full name written in her chicken-scratch scrawl. I laugh. A whole season gone by, and she simply named the eagle after me in the end.

I smooth out the creases in the paper. From it, I fold my last star. This one needs no incantation. My name is a spell, one that I can cast because I am only human, and another human being has written it in gratitude, and there is nothing more powerful than that.

It's finally night. I gather all my stars, hundreds of them in my arms, and I step out into the courtyard. There is a fresh carpet of autumn leaves at my feet. I feel like I'm floating on a brilliant sea of red, and as I walk out of the temple grounds and down the mountain slope, I open my arms. The stars soar skywards, one by one. They are lighting up the dark, first with brightness, then warmth. An incredible warmth. I know this warmth will reach the city. I know Sun will feel it, but most of all, I know my father will feel it. And he will know that I live, that he cannot hurt me anymore, and that there will be peace when we reach the city.

"Sunshade, Starlight"

CUIFEN CHEN is working towards her MA in Creative Writing in Singapore, but has spent many years abroad in the UK and Australia. Her poetry has appeared in the *Southeast Asian Review of English*, and in 2018 she was the first prize winner of the UK's Troubadour International Poetry Prize. "Sunshade, Starlight" is her first published story, and the winner of this year's Literary Taxidermy Short Story Competition. We loved the story's setting, the tension between the characters, and of course the idea of magical papercraft. It was a thrill to read and a pleasure to award.

She says: "It was Qing Ming season when I discovered the Literary Taxidermy competition. Qing Ming is when we remember ancestors by visiting the temple and burning paper offerings, so when I saw the words *It was a pleasure to burn*, that was what came to me immediately. A girl in a temple, burning a paper offering. Who she was, and why she was doing that, took more than a month to get onto paper, but that opening image was vivid from the start."

Mado Yatta

Hell Yes!

IT WAS A PLEASURE TO BURN, thinks Spicy Alice. It had, after all, been a very long time since anything—or anyone—had made her feel quite so *good.* Which is what happens when you are forty-two and the vast majority of men you attract are cargo cultists or momma's boys, imbeciles or innocents, who are, quite frankly, more likely to find God in your panties than your clitoris; and the men in her office were even worse, and every one of them as boring in the bedroom as in the boardroom. Whoever said the hallmark of heaven was an angelic choir of ennui was right. The spawn of the devil, she'd tell her girlfriends, that's what she needed—the spawn of the devil.

Spicy Alice—that wasn't her real name, of course. No good Catholic mother would ever name her daughter "Spicy Alice." But in the digital age you can name yourself anything, and it was Spicy Alice that stuck. Just the right combination of empowerment and availability, she thought, and thus her *alter ego* was born—although honestly there was very little *altar* about it. So now, when Alice starts her bright-red Audi A3 in the shared garage under her apartment in Mid-City Santa Monica, a low British voice growls, "Good morning, Spicy Alice," and while most mornings the greeting conjures in her mind images of rough & ready London boys, this morning it's a bit more English lord & branding iron. She pulls her hands from the wheel and presses the button just under the dashboard. The car falls back asleep. She eyes the cross dangling from her review mirror—a gift from her mother last Easter. She's not going anywhere, not yet. She needs a moment, maybe two, to pull herself together, to think, to *imagine*. She places a hand on her thigh, feels the tautness of her size-six jeans, runs a red fingernail over the denim. Her pants are so tight she can barely move—and if she can be still, really still, and if she can concentrate, focus, she can feel *his* fingers on her hips.

Ping!

It's Alice's phone. She glances at the text. *Well damn!* she thinks. S*peak of the devil.* Her mind jumps back to the party. She'd arrived hungry, but without much hope, and after a few cocktails paired with pricey *hors d'oeuvres* and stilted conversation, she'd retreated to the library to smoke a joint, maybe undo a button or two and then try her luck again, and that's when he found her. Tall, dark, handsome, and dressed in fifty shades of black. *A bit of a Goth cliché*, she'd thought, but it worked. She'd tried to guess his age, but it was impossible; and his eyes burned with a timeless intensity—and when he stepped closer, right into her personal space, and when those eyes met her own, his gaze didn't just pierce her, it opened her completely. He introduced himself as Mantus. Weird name. It made her think of "praying mantis." She asked if he was an actor, and he laughed. Lawyer? "I am Mantus," he said again, this time with a slight curl to his lips, as if amused. "This country is planted thick with lawyers, from coast to coast, don't you think?" His accent, like his appearance, was an adjective overload; deep and dark, silky and sibilant, and hard to pin down. Then he took her hand, leaned closer, and whispered, "I am also known as the Etruscan god of Hell"—which was an odd thing to say—and she'd been in LA long enough to have more than passing familiarity with odd. And his grip— dear God! It was hot, *literally* hot, like a stove. She jerked her hand away, and then felt a sudden chill go through her. No, not a chill, exactly; more like a shiver, as if every nerve in her body had suddenly jumped to life, demanding that she get that fire back!

She takes a deep breath and reads his text again:

Today at 6:54 am

Alice smiles, remembering. Yes, ok, it's true. She won't deny it. Last night she had indeed *fucked* the Devil. It was hard to believe—she couldn't quite believe it herself—and she sure as hell hadn't expected to hear from him again. In fact, she wasn't sure she wanted to hear from him at all. There was a lot to process about last night. You'd think sex with the Devil was all black leather and whips in dark dungeons, but Alice learned that Satan was more into satin, or, at least, high-thread count cotton sheets. And there was no denying he was…well, *hot stuff*. But fucking the Devil *once* is one thing—did she really want this to be a regular event? Alice's eyes grow wide in thought, and she can see her mother frowning at the sacrilegious visions racing through her head. Still, there was really only one answer: *Hell yes!*

In the library, Spicy Alice undid another button on her blouse—casually, she'd hoped, but the gesture was as practiced as it was premeditated. Mantus said something about "the doors of perception" and "the key to intimacy," and that was enough to get things rolling. They returned to the bar in the living room and sipped Manhattans and suddenly they were discussing life, and love, and loss. A lawyer from her firm cut in, and the conversation veered disappointingly from flirtation and personal history to the undermining of the judiciary and national politics. Alice knew what that meant. She'd spent too many hours at the tail-end of parties locked into these same anaphrodisiacal laments with all sorts of men. Didn't anyone just want to fuck anymore?!? She took a deep breath and forced a smile, bracing herself for a long conversation and another lonely night. But it was different with Mantus. The conversation sparked something in him. He was thoughtful about the state of the world but not depressed by it. In fact, just the opposite. "Bad people do good things all the time," he said, draping an arm over Alice's shoulder and leading her away from the interloping lawyer with a nod. "And some people are as likely to serve God, without intending it, as the Devil." They found their next round of drinks and he asked, "Have you ever done something so bad it made your heart flutter?" And then: "Do you remember, as a child, the pleasure of knocking down a stack of blocks? Of throwing a piece of wood onto the fire and watching it burn?" They walked and talked, moving from living room to deck, and then deck to poolside with a beautiful view from the Hollywood Hills down into the city. She kicked off her shoes and dangled her feet in the water. He sat beside her, legs crossed. There was something about this guy, this Mantus. He didn't seem like a Goth, but what was an "Etruscan," anyway? The party buzz was cooling down with the night, but she just kept warming up. When he dipped a hand into the water, it seemed to bubble all around him. She suggested they might want to find another spot. A *private* spot. She moved in closer so they were touching, shoulder to shoulder. In the coolness of the night air, she could feel his warmth again. It was like sitting by a fire. When Spicy Alice at last leaned in and kissed him—a big, full, open mouth kiss—he responded enthusiastically, and his tongue slipped between her lips. It was hotter than his hand, if that was possible, and she felt like she was being licked by flame. She gasped, "Just who the hell are you?"

"Like I said, Alice, I'm Mantus, the Etruscan god of Hell. And I'd like to take you home tonight."

Spicy Alice stood and shook the water from her feet, then slipped on her shoes. "I don't know," she teased. "Shouldn't a man's reach always exceed his grasp?" Mantus rose, his movements fluid and easy, like a dancer's. "A man's reach, perhaps," he said. "But a woman's? I wager you may grasp anything you'd like tonight."

"What would *you* like to grasp tonight?"

He waved his hand towards the city below. "Let me take you—"

"Take me?"

"Let me take you home tonight."

"Home?"

"To Hell."

"But I love LA."

Mantus gestured towards the city again. "Heaven, Hell, LA—it's really one and the same." Alice didn't quite know how to respond to that, but she raised her Manhattan in agreement anyway, and toasted.

"To Hell," she said.

"To Hell," he agreed.

They clinked glasses.

Ping!

It's another text. The Devil is into details, apparently.

How about a morning ride?
Today at 6:55 am

🚗 or 🐐 —your choice.
Today at 6:55 am

She glances up into the rear-view mirror. Checks her hair, her lipstick. Then her watch. She *really* has to get to work, doesn't she? The 405 could be a creeping purgatory if she waits much longer, she might arrive late to work, the Jensen case might be back on her desk, Natalie might corner her again for lunch. And yet there *he* is—right now—in that blue bubble on her phone, waiting for her to reply. The Devil she knows. She stares at his text, thinking, calculating, stalling before her reply. *Imagining*. She feels the pull to obey, to answer his call. But what do you say when the Devil wants to take you out for a spin? Last night when they had reached his place, a surprisingly small apartment in the heart of the city, things went from baking to blazing. At first, his touched warmed, then tingled, and, finally, burned. She wanted to scream, but the only thing that came out of her mouth was a long, deep moan of pleasure. Mantus lifted his fingers from her naked hip, and Spicy Alice looked at where he'd touched her. Five red welts had appeared. "What the fuck?" She was panting. *Who the hell are you?* she'd asked earlier, but that was flirting. Now she was serious. She *needed* to know. She looked around, looking for clues. His apartment was small, but neat. Books everywhere. A few posters on his walls. A simple kitchenette. Nothing too revealing, but everything real. His bedroom was much the same. They were on his bed, her tiny black skirt hiked up. His hand, still hovering above her skin, radiating heat from his barely raised fingers, and she longed for him to touch her again. To burn her. To *brand* her. Mantus looked a little bored as he repeated: "I'm Mantus, the Etruscan god of Hell." His eyes flashed as they had done before, and again she felt pierced—and filled—by his light. She thought of Prometheus, bringing fire to mankind. Then of Lucifer, bringer of light. Then her thoughts became muddled, and the yearning overwhelmed everything. She let her hip rise slightly, just grazing the fingertips of his hand. There was another delicate *hisssss* as skin began to burn. She could smell her own flesh-smoke. She struggled to get the next few words out. "So…you're telling me…I'm about…to fuck an actual demon?"

"Demon?" He sounded insulted.

"A devil, then?"

"Not a devil, my dear," Mantus said. "*The* Devil."

Alice looked hard at him. Where were the horns, the cloven hooves? And what was the Devil doing in the City of Angels, anyway? In God's country.

He laughed. "God's country?"

"This—this is nuts," she said.

"*La plus belle des ruses du Dieu est de vous persuader qu'il existe.*"

"What?"

Mantus pulled her close, hips to hips, and then lips to lips. Everything sizzled. "The Devil's just another angel," Mantus whispered. He put a warm hand between her legs. She opened wider willingly, his hand grew hotter, and that's when she started coming.

She couldn't remember when she stopped.

Ping!

Play hooky 🐎, call in sick 😷, tell them the Devil 😈 made you do it!

Today at 6:56 am

She regards the cross hanging from her rearview mirror. She thinks of Sundays at the United Episcopal in Pittsburgh—all that cursing at devils, evil, and sin. Really, what was that all about? All that denial, stuffing your life into an empty little box. Did she buy any of it? Did she—in her heart of hearts—really stand against *anything*? She shakes her head, unsure. But a glance back at her phone reminds her what she stands *for*: the pleasure of that burn. She texts, "Come for me," and there is a sudden screech of tires. A car has pulled up in front of hers, a dingy blue Acura Integra, spewing exhaust. A lot of exhaust. She checks her seatbelt, grabs her phone. She opens her door and exits her Audi, but wow that exhaust is everywhere, a thick white cloud, rising around her ankles, her hips. Before she takes two steps, it's over her head, a total white-out, and she has to place a hand on her car for guidance. She walks slowly towards the only thing she can see: the soft red glow from the Integra's taillights. When she reaches his car, the passenger door opens, as if by magic.

"It's good to see you again," says Mantus as she climbs in. The door closes behind her. She coughs once or twice, and he laughs. He's wearing the same clothes as the night before—black on black—and she feels just as hungry, eager, and ready. The air conditioner is running and the interior of the car is cool. Mantus makes a small gesture with the index finger of his right hand, a tiny flick towards the top button of her blouse, and she knows right away what she wants to do. What she's always wanted to do. She starts to undress. It takes a while to squirm her way out of her jeans, but squirm she does; and it feels good to be naked, so good. Spicy Alice bunches up and then tosses her clothes into the back seat, but not before noticing the dozens of other blouses and jeans, bras and socks, t-shirts, stockings, and panties back there.

"Where to?" Mantus says. He revs the engine several times. Alice looks from Mantus out into the garage, now completely obscured by the thick fog of exhaust. *Where to? Where to?* She slides back into her seat. *Well, that's easy!* "Straight to Hell," says Alice with a glint in her eye. "Take me *now!*" Spicy Alice pulls the seat belt tight over her naked hips and straps herself in, but Mantus shakes his head. He reaches over and unbuckles her. He punches the accelerator and the car jumps, full speed ahead, straight into the impenetrable fog.

"When we reach the city, baby, when we reach the city!"

"Hell Yes!"

MADO YATTA is a surveyor at Materials Laboratory in Kentucky, in the United States. In her spare time, she's a volunteer groom at Churchill Downs, home of the famous Kentucky Derby. "Hell Yes!" is her third published short story.

She says: "I love horses and wanted to write a story that captured a feeling of coltish impatience. Throw in a little bit of good and evil and God and the devil, and the story just took off. It was fun to play with these ideas and to create a character and story that had an edgy and slightly ambiguous spirit of adventure and freedom."

Alexander Christian Lwin

Spark

IT WAS A PLEASURE TO BURN. Nothing else felt quite like it. Nothing felt as visceral, as vibrant, as real to Pogo. He loved it. He loved the way his skin tightened, twisted and constricted. How it snapped and flaked in the flames. How the sclera of his eyes ran down his face in thick and sticky tears. He loved the tingling and he loved the warmth. He loved how it cocooned him, caressed him, and hurt him. It was a partner, a parent, and a punishment all at once. It was what made him special, and it was his own personal miracle.

From the moment he was born, he was remarkable. No matter what damage was inflicted upon his body, he would heal without so much as a scar. That's why it didn't matter that he grew up stupid. Nor that he grew up ugly, short, fat, and squat. His unique skill washed over all his imperfections, and by the time he exited adolescence and entered adulthood he'd found his place as a performer.

In the heart of the city of dreams and vice, in The Pyre snugly fit in the bosom of Las Vegas, the show begins every Sunday night. The circus runs to the beat of the band and the crowd leans in as the entertainer makes his entrance. He waves to the crowd and greedily pours gasoline over himself. The liquid sinks into every pore, fills his eyes and nose, and makes itself at home. And then the spotlight comes on. The snare drum plays its roll. He takes a golden lighter to a lock of greasy hair. His wick. And the rolling fat of his body becomes a wax candle to a red-hot flame. In that moment, he is a star. Burning brightly, the smoky scent of burning hair and skin fills the room but the audience is too drunk on mayhem to mind. They gasp and jeer and laugh as he runs around to a frantic blaring of trumpets and kazoo. They go silent as the clowns put out the roaming candle, watching it collapse to the floor in a blackened mess. And, finally, they cheer and clap once more as the naked corpse, burnt and blind, leaps to its feet. Flesh sloughing off its bones in charcoal heaps, it takes its bow and dances around. How they all hoot and holler, how they cackle at the surreal sight. And when the curtain drops on another success, Pogo's body begins to heal itself in preparation for next week's show.

One day, a great magician appeared before Pogo and the theatre manager. He called himself Paskunji, claimed he had travelled the world learning how to master the art of miracles. He'd trekked through desert and rainforest and up mountains and down the abyss. He'd spoken to starving children who persisted for days without food, he'd talked to drowning sailors living at the bottom of the sea, he'd spoken to shambling men who lived with hollowed out caverns where their insides should be. He had, or so he claimed, undone the illusion of life and now it was all laid as bare as an overturned card.

If nothing else, Paskunji had showmanship. He could spin a story. The manager appreciated that, even if Pogo didn't. The manager bid him, let's see what you can do, and he waved the magician onto the stage, taking his place within the gallery.

Drumroll.

The magician started with a few card tricks. Sleight of hand, picking a predetermined card, other mundane feats of magic. Pogo was unimpressed, the manager even less so. Next, the magician began performing some simple illusions. Disappearing acts, escape artistry, making things appear and disappear. By now, the manager was yawning and Pogo was silently laughing. The magician had made an ass of himself. For all his talk, his routine was stale. Forgettable. Just another farce before the crowd.

Ladies and gentlemen, Paskunji thanked his judges, I have one final act for you today. He gently removed his hat and cape, his jacket and gloves, his glasses and tie. Unmarred by lenses, his eyes are bright and dewy. His smile is the carefree grin of a child. Everything is silent now. Not just the audience, but the air itself. The crickets and flies and roaches have all stopped and turned to watch Paskunji's magic. He retrieves a thick metal drum of oil and heaves it up above his head. His legs pull apart and his knees buckle as he gets into position, he licks his lips in anticipation. It's show time. A waterfall of oil pours from the drum and cascades across Paskunji's form. Drained and empty, he effortlessly tosses the drum away. As it bounces away, every strike to the metal rings out across the theatre. Next, he picks up a match and strikes it across the stage. It sparks and light and shadow play across his face as he raises it towards the sky. A glistening, flammable, statue of liberty. He stands still but for a moment. He soaks up the trepidation, lets it fuel the beating of his heart. And then, when he can see the fear in the viewers' eyes, he lets the match drop.

It spins in midair. A graceful swan dive into a murky pool. The moment before impact, it freezes. Dangles in the air.

Then everything ignites. Arms held out, a ball of fire burning blue sparks explodes from the human firework. He is a supernova. He flashes for a moment, cloth and skin fuse together and fade away. He crumbles and burns like paper. Piece by piece, Paskunji breaks away until there is nothing left to find. A charred smear, a mark of ash, left upon the stage. But nothing remotely human. With the fire still burning, the curtain drops.

From behind the curtain something stirs. Rising slowly, a figure painstakingly re-builds itself from the soot and ash. Feet. Legs. A body with arms and hands attached. Finally, a head. And when the curtain rises, he is reborn. Yes, unmarred and alive, stands Paskunji in the flesh.

He bows. And the audience applauds.

Pogo had never seen something so beautiful in his life. Which is why it was so terrible. So disgusting. So heart wrenching and brutal. To see someone who did what he loved, what he was supposed to be the one to do, and did it far better…. Everything rose within Pogo. Blood, acid and bile. It all froths to the surface and crushes his brain to a messy pulp. And jealousy, a previously unfamiliar emotion, wells in Pogo and takes flight.

The lights go off.

Hours later, Pogo finds himself in his room. Doubled-over, stained shirt, he may have been drinking but he doesn't know. There's blood in his head, but none on his hands. Fever. Delirium. Poison running in his veins. Caged in his skull, grey matter pounds and beats on the walls of its cell. He stares at the ceiling and the ceiling averts its eyes.

Oh, Lord. He begs. Why would you take this from me? Living is a curse, but for my meagre miracle. What, then, am I to do now? You have stolen from me my only flame. It hurts. It pains me more than any agony I have endured. Every scar I have neglected throbs within. And I ask you again, why? I have not demanded much of you. I have been content! I did not desire to be the best at everything. Hell, I did not ask to even be good at most things. All I wished, all I have ever pleaded, was that I be the best at one thing. Only one. That I be allowed to have talent. And now you have taken that from me. How could you let another exist? How could you rob me of my reason to be?

But there was no answer. Because there didn't need to be an answer. Warm droplets of liquid dribbled down Pogo's face, and his blood boiled. He found his own answer in the silence, crafted his own divine inspiration. Paskunji, Pogo decided, was cheating.

Paskunji hadn't been *chosen*. He was a fraud.

Once he came to that realisation, it all clicked into place. The need for the curtain to fall. The turning to ash. The removal of his costume. Every detail became a clue strung up on the corkboard of a fervent mind. Paskunji's abilities were an illusion. A trick. A lie. Pogo detested him for it, for he knew that before the eyes of an adoring audience any scam is just as good as the real thing. There was nothing left to it. Pogo found his resolve. Paskunji must return to the hell from which all devils come.

Almost dawn. The corridors of the theatre are empty. Not even dust chooses to linger past closing time. Only Pogo. Pogo knows that the frequent and the new performers always lodge in the theatre. He also knows that the newest performer is always given the room at the end of the corridor, on the left, by the stacked boxes of outdated props. That box would be his armoury, Pogo decides, drawing a heavy metal bat as his sword. He weighs it, checks the heft; it's solid and has a lovely swing. Pogo smiles wide. The kind of smile that a baby makes before it learns happiness. He runs his fingers around the bronze lining of the door handle, teasing it, before grabbing it and turning. Unlocked. Reality is slipping, he holds back a fit of giggles and slips into the room. Stalking his way to the foot of the bed, creeping like a shadow out of place. He is shorter than Paskunji by many feet, but now he feels like he towers over the other man. A swaying spire; tower of babel. All messy edges, wobbling and teetering on the brink of collapse, but firm all the same. He is suddenly acutely aware of the weight of the bat as he wields it overhead. It threatens to slip out of his grip. But even now, Paskunji sleeps.

The bat swings down and Paskunji's china-plate skull cracks open. A grim orifice spilling warm droplets of bloody sponge like cockroaches bursting forth. Ecstasy. Climax. Pogo had never felt this before. Nothing so visceral. Nothing so vibrant. He swings it again and shatters bone. He swings it again and violets bloom on pale skin. He swings it again and he almost feels real. He loves it. He loves how it sprays upon his skin. He loves how it cracks and bursts. He loves how everything makes sense once more. He wants to be a beast, to become a lion like in a fairytale, to discard his bat and tear apart his prey. He wants to go feral.

But he keeps swinging in silence. His expression never changing, a grim stone mask of determination. He is a human furnace, he is an oven burning bone and blood, only the glow of his eyes and the heat of his flesh let slip the fire within. Thick plumes of smoke exhale from his maw in ragged breaths. It feels like hours pass. Or maybe seconds. His arms grow tired and he drops the bat. It splashes in the bedside pool. Show's over. Time to clean up.

Even now the dull thud of drums beats over and over again in his ear, but he ignores it. He opens the magician's trunk and clears it out. Then he ladles its former owner inside the makeshift coffin. Using the bedsheets and some bleach he finds in the bathroom, he carefully wipes up all the spillage and tosses the sheets into the trunk. He throws the bat in for good measure too. Now that the room is clean, he needs to clean himself. He washes up in Paskunji's shower, cool droplets hissing and evaporating upon his body. Then, once all the blood and grime is gone, he grabs a costume from the box outside (an orangutang) and dresses himself. His previous clothes and the towel could be DNA evidence, so they go in the trunk as well. Taking one last thorough sweep of the room, he is finally satisfied.

It's early morning now. People are waking up, but no-one even seems to notice the monkey driving with a trunk in his backseat. They have no incentive to look. Pogo drives for miles, passing the city limits. But still he drives on. The rest of the theatre must be waking up now, he figures. But still he drives on. Sand covers the road and sprays against his windshield. But still he drives on. Into the desert, away from anywhere that could implicate him, he drives. And finally, not a soul in sight, he stops and gets out of the car. Droplets of sweat ooze from his head and his palms, and flies dance within his sight. He heaves out the heavy trunk and drags it away from the car. He fans himself with his hand to cool down, but the morning sun is relentless in its judgement. Whatever. Things are about to get much hotter. Pogo opens the boot of the car and pulls out his lighter and gas can.

If they can't connect the body to me, he mumbles as mantra, *they can't connect the murder to me*. Like seasoning a salad, or putting on cologne, he splashes the trunk and all its contents with gasoline. Splash. Splash. Splash. He douses it all to the very last drop. And then, the sun glinting off his lighter, he starts his wicked bonfire.

The fire dances for Pogo in a white hot inferno, and so he wants to dance too. It flickers and celebrates and eats with a ravenous appetite. It's a black hole that devours everything. And Pogo is pleased. He loves it. He loves the way the corpse's skin crackles, bubbles and pops. How bone chars and crumbles in the flame. How the heat causes droplets to run down his face in soft and stinging tears. With blurred eyes, he watches his senses and jealousy and doubts and inadequacies all burn away in place of his guilt, for he has none. And once only smoke and ash is left, Pogo climbs back into his car and turns the radio and air-con on. He wipes the dashboard of condensation and his face of soot, and begins to drive back home.

And as he drives away, far away from what he has done, somewhere on the blackened hot sands of the desert, flesh mends and muscle knits and a fresh coat of skin crawls back over a body. But Pogo doesn't know this. And as the buildings come into view, he melts into his seat. We'll be fine, he assures himself, we'll be safe. It'll be over, when we reach the city.

"Spark"

ALEXANDER CHRISTIAN LWIN is an Australian post-graduate. "Spark" is his first published short story.

He says: "When I was a child, I lived in a house haunted by three ghosts. I wish I could say it made me better at writing horror, but it turns out most ghosts are pretty boring. They just float around and watch you sleep. The second I read the prompt for this competition, however, the perfect scene popped into my head. The tough part was trying to create a whole story to justify it. In the end, despite having lived with actual ghosts, I still had to turn to horror fiction for ideas. I can't help but feel a little ripped off!"

Erika Bauer

A Dark and Final Space

IT WAS A PLEASURE TO BURN. That first sip like coming home, she thought, burning out all the old thoughts, replacing them with that calm emptiness, that final shrug of the shoulders that lays it all down.

"Again," she said to the bartender. "Please," she added. "Again, *please*."

The bartender poured another bourbon. All the old clichés were in place: a dimly lit bar dotted by wet rings from happier times, a woman staring into a glass, her mascara just beginning to do the night-time fade into the corners of her eyes, a spattering of men of indeterminate age sunk into barstools and back corners. It was Hemingway without the clean, well-lightedness.

"Let me guess," the bartender said. "A guy, right?" He was older than the woman at the bar by some marginal amount that daylight might reveal. He used the towel in his hands to wipe the wet rings away, his hands moving in a circular, hypnotic motion. "You can tell me. Attorney-client privilege, am I right?" He smiled at her but she didn't see it. Her eyes were on the glass.

The woman didn't want to answer but she knew that not answering was also an answer. She could tell him to mind his damn business, she could smile and remain quiet, she could lie and tell him she lost her job. In the end though, she was tired and she kept it simple.

"He's leaving," she said simply. "He's leaving and it's too late." The bartender nodded like he already knew.

"Yup," he said. "Heard that one before. 'Cept, it's never *too* late, you know? I mean, it can be 'late,' but there's never a 'too late.' Not ever." He laid out a row of wet shot glasses and began to dry them. Somewhere in the back of the bar, darts softly sailed through the air, each one hitting the target with a precise exhalation. A man alone at a table began to slump down, allowing the alcohol to take him the rest of the way to that goodnight.

"It's too late," she said. "He got a new job, in a new city. He sold his apartment. And I didn't say a thing, you know? Not one goddamn thing. Not one, 'Hey, you know, by the way, I sort of love you, I think. I sort of want you to stay. I sort of want....'" She imagined her hands on the back of his neck, that part of a man's neck where the hair is cut close and feels so pretty if you run your fingers through it. So shallow. Like waves.

Her eyes met the bartender's. "Well, you know what I want," she trailed off. He nodded slowly, more than once, enough to clearly say how much he knew.

He set a napkin down on the bar. "Write it down," he said. "Write down what you would have said to him. If you had had the chance, you know?" She looked at him, the mascara of her right eye now beyond the point of repair. "It will help. Scout's honor."

It was such a funny thing to say in a place like this, a dark place, a place where people swallowed feelings, and forced their hands to steady, and pretended that the laughter coming from their mouths didn't also sound a bit like screams, a bit like tears. She almost waited for him to raise his right hand, scout's honor and all. Instead he pushed the napkin closer. "Go on," he said.

"Another bourbon," she said. He nodded his head, poured the bourbon, and set a pen down next to the napkin.

"Real fucking funny," she said. She wanted it to sound forceful, but it didn't. It came out too rehearsed, too detached. She was already beginning to think about the pen and the napkin and the note. She was already imagining herself mailing it later that night—just walking up to the blue box at 2:30 a.m. and stuffing it in an envelope and grabbing a stamp and dropping it into the box before she had time to think.

The bartender picked up the dried shot glasses and walked to the other end of the counter.

The pen sat there waiting. The man at the table behind her continued his alcoholic slumber, alone in his booth. The dart players finished their game and asked for another round of beers.

She picked up the pen. She stretched out the napkin. For an entire year, she had watched him arrive in the morning to work, the five minute window of his arrival a kind of religion. It was something she'd never admit, how she wouldn't leave her desk during those five minutes or she might miss the first glimpse of him walking down the hall. Sometimes she would try to arrange a pretense for passing him in the hallway, like making copies at the exact moment she heard his footsteps approaching. Other times she would wrack her mind for some bit of work-related conversation that she could use just to watch his eyes hear her words, just long enough to pretend they were talking about something less forced.

The napkin on the bar began to absorb a wet spot beneath it. It soaked up the water in a small circle, one less place for her to put down the words that were escaping her.

His office was on the floor above her. Her door was near the stairwell so it was impossible for him to come down without passing by her door. Sometimes she pretended an errand to walk past his door, looking but not looking at him at his desk as she wasted yet another opportunity.

And then one day, as she was making copies, he came in. Just the two of them. He smiled at her. She smiled back.

"I'm almost done," she said to him. He didn't know that she wanted to make copies forever. He didn't know that she was watching the way he wrote so neatly on the paper in his hand, the way he always did. His letters perfect blocks. Hands she wanted to touch just once.

"No rush. To tell you the truth, this is my last day, so ahh…yeah…no rush, you know?" He smiled again.

"Your last day?"

"Yeah," he said. "I got a job in the city. Advertising for Howard & Klein. A real big opportunity, you know? Something I've been waiting for my whole life. I've always wanted to live in the city; I've always wanted to hear what they mean by 'it never sleeps.'"

"The city? Wow. That's quite a step up." She used her brain to form a smile she couldn't feel.

"Yeah, I feel like things are going to change, you know? I'm going to finally be where I belong. I'm going to have a whole new life. I don't know; I sound like a kid, huh? But, man, when I reach the city…."

At the bar, the woman downed the last bit of bourbon glistening in the bottom of the glass. She watched a man and a woman making out in a booth to her right, the woman putting her leg over his, his hand locked on the back of her neck, the darkness keeping it all together and pretty and real. The bartender was talking to an old man on an end barstool. They were laughing about something—a dirty joke, a nagging wife at home, another whiskey.

She picked up the pen and wrote what she wanted to say on the napkin. It was simple, the way that truth is. The words came quickly and she didn't need much space. She thought of his face and all the times she tried to catch his eyes, and all the days she wished she had told him that she loved him before she knew him, and all the dreams she had of brushing the back of his hand. She thought of the number of hours in between the wanting, all the ways she could have used those minutes, all the conversations she could have had. The pen did feel good in her hand. It did feel better to write this down, at this place, alone, on a napkin that would soon be crumbled up in the bottom of a 2 a.m. garbage can.

When she was done, she laid the pen down, put a $20 on the table for the bartender, and walked out into the night. As she walked from relative darkness to relative darkness, she thought about his smile, the muscles at the back of his neck, the way his voice would always sound, where he might be right now, in that city, someplace, with someone, the way his eyes lit up when he said, "When I reach the city." All that that meant.

Her own apartment was just two blocks away. She let it hurt all the way home. She thought about the napkin on the bar. She imagined where they could have been if only this were a story....

As the bartender flashed the lights signaling last call, the woman was just unlocking her front door. He gathered up the remaining glasses, cashed out the final patrons, and walked back over to the pen. The napkin had not been folded; it lay facing him, red ink a bit crooked from the bourbon, but mostly all intact.

He picked up the note, the note from the woman to the man that would never be sent. It seemed ok to read it, so he did. It was short. He folded up the napkin and put it in his pocket. It didn't seem right to throw it away.

He turned off the lights in the bar and locked the door. He touched the napkin in his pocket and thought about the words. He thought maybe he'd dream of them tonight, whatever they meant.

When we reach the city, she had written in red ink, with a mostly steady hand. *When we reach the city*.

"A Dark and Final Space"

ERIKA BAUER is a teacher in Michigan, in the United States. She's a closet 80's rock karaoke super star, and if she could live anywhere, it would be in Castle Rock (even though it's fictional). She owns four turtles that yawn like lions when no one is looking and aspires to write the way that Muhammad Ali boxed. "A Dark and Final Space" is her first published short story.

She says: "I knew from the first line that the story would be set in a bar, that the woman in the bar would be alone, and that everything in between should feel as close to Hemingway as I could channel. Getting to that final line, though, was difficult. I gave up more than once. I even tried to delete the bar itself! No go. Honestly, the story wrote itself."

A. M. Metivier

Jane Austen Sucks

IT WAS A PLEASURE TO BURN. Maybe, it shouldn't have been. Maybe the pleasure of burning Schuyler's stuff was the reason my step-father Dutch was driving me to Saint Dymphna Hospital, so far north it might as well have been in Canada. I guess that's the way it goes. Gotta go into a box and let them run me through the maze. I'm just a mouse to be studied, and fed to the cat. Squeak. Squeak.

Besides, it wasn't like Schuyler was going to miss his stuff. His Boston Lawyer pater would buy him more. That's how it worked with rich people. Get rid of the mess. Don't discuss it. Don't worry about Harvard because if the legacy doesn't get you in, the donation will. Every rich guy slums it at least once.

Exuli exilium imperas nec das. Medea knew her shit.

I was probably doing Boston Lawyer a favor. Saved him from a feckless musician son. Maybe instead of a guitar, he would buy Schuy a new car. Oh, the punishments of the rich.

It's pretty in spring. Everything green and filled with promise rushing past the window. I see wild onions. Can't miss them, so tall and green where the grass is short and yellow. I want to grab them and eat them and go to St Dymphna smelling of an old Hungarian woman. Maybe I'll speak in an accent to prove how crazy I am.

Nah. Too cuckoo.

Still, I wish I could pick the onions. They won't help me though.

My step-dad won't stop. Probably not even if I say I have to pee. Well, maybe if I have to pee.

Why did Schuyler tell me to call?

A touch of guilt? Wouldn't that be great! Guilt for the guileless Schuyler! Something to make him think of me. Something to make him remember. Something to make him hurt.

I don't know how this works. Will they put me in a padded cell? Guess I'm lucky I wasn't arrested. That's what my advisor said. Boston Lawyer's not pressing charges. Boston Lawyer could make things really bad for me. Boston Lawyer is merciful.

Unlike his son.

Who told me to call.

I couldn't find Dymphna in my book of saints. Picked the book up to annoy my mom. Guess she was right. It *was* useless. *Obscurum sanctus* is our little Santa Dymphna. I left all my books behind. They, like guitars, can burn. Don't want to rock the straightjacket boat.

"Can I open the window?"

"Sure. Just don't do anything stupid." That's Dutch. He really hates me. I'm not sure if I hate him, too. I mean, he treats Mom alright. He handles stuff she can't handle. He hates me because my shitty little drama is making her upset. I think Dutch is really scared of Boston Lawyer.

So I open the window. Just a little bit.

I wonder if Dutch will go back and get the rest of my stuff. Doesn't matter. I'm the financial aid kid in the hall. No Laura Ashley here, thank you. None of those brats want my low rent junk. Except maybe the "Toothpaste Princess." She steals crap all the time. Her family has a product in half the mouths in America, and she needs to steal socks and cassette tapes to feel alive. Everyone knows she does it. She's been caught like six times. She gets private counseling and a single room. Me, I get sent to Saint Dymphna for a little fire on the JV soccer field.

First lesson of Private Prep: Rich people can do whatever the fuck they want.

Schuyler did.

No one sending him away.

I put my head against the window and breathe. The air smells of…exhaust, Dutch's cigarettes, and the cinnamon pine tree hanging from the rear view. I see if I can pick out the smell of spring from outside. I want to smell the wet dirt and old leaves. Is it there?

In my mind, I see a place in the woods under the shelter of trees. The air is damp. I see clouds scuttle across blue sky. It smells of verdurous earth. There's a memory in this soft and shaded spot that makes me feel hollow.

"If we stop, are you gonna do something stupid?" Dutch asks.

"Like what? Shoot Reagan again?"

"Always a goddam joke with you. I'm serious. If I pull over, are you gonna do something stupid because I swear to Christ I will piss in a bottle and keep this goddam car on the road if I think for a second you're gonna do something stupid."

"Yeah, yeah, the president's safe."

"Always a goddam joke…" he mumbles while pulling off the highway into the parking lot of a diner. The place is blue, white, and made of metal. He's still mumbling when we step inside.

He puts his coat over a stool at the counter. "Sit down," he says. He turns to the waitress walking over, "I'll get a black coffee, two eggs sunny side-up, bacon and home fries, and rye toast dark. Get the kid what she wants, but don't let her order anything crazy." Then, he follows the arrow marked restrooms and leaves me.

The waitress is not too old and wears her hair in a ponytail. "What can I get you?" she asks.

"Another life?"

She stares at me in a way that says she's contemplating spitting in my food.

"Sorry," I sit down, "Just white toast, please. No butter."

"You want dry toast?" Her penciled eyebrows raise as if I've just asked her to give me the cook's head on a platter.

"Yes, please." I'm thirsty and want water, but I'm too scared she's going to spit in it.

They have a payphone near the door. I have a lot of quarters. I took those with me. I had them for the washing machines at school. I wonder if I should call Schuyler and tell him I am here. That I'm O.K.

What is wrong with me? He doesn't care. He's probably laughing with all of his jerk-bag friends. Would calling him make him suffer? Would it make him sorry?

Probably not. I'm below his regard.

Right?

I mean, does he care about me? He asked me to call him, to use a different name so no one would know it was me. That means he cares, right?

But why can't I use my name?

Dutch returns and sits down on top of his coat. The waitress brings his coffee as if she didn't trust me alone with it. He's quiet, staring at the milk shake machine. I start tearing the paper placemat into squares. I can tell he hates it, but he's not saying anything. By the time I have made a small stack of paper squares, the waitress comes with our food.

"That all you're eating?" he asks.

"I'm on the arson diet."

He drops the fork and knife on his plate, making a noise louder than I thought silverware could. His face is frozen mid-chew, like his eggs and potatoes turned to cement.

"Sorry," I say. And you know what, I really am. I mean, I get that he hates me, but he is here. He's cleaning up a mess I made. He's making a bed I keep struggling to sleep in.

He takes a deep breath and sighs. "I'm gonna ask you a question, and I don't want any jokes from you, OK?"

"OK."

"What did that boy do? I want you to be honest with me. Why'd you burn his stuff?"

"I don't know—"

"Damnit, don't lie to me!" His hands are fists. Is he going to murder Schuyler if I tell him?

"I gotta go to the bathroom." I walk fast, almost run into the hall leading to a door marked "Ladies." I go inside and lock the door. I feel like there's a strap around my chest, like I'm going to stop breathing. I hear a ringing in my ears and tears are coming out of me and they just won't stop.

And then I'm on the floor, holding my knees, back braced against the door to save me from my fuck-up. To save me from it all.

How the fuck did I let this happen?

Jesus, why did I believe fucking Jane Austen and all of her love-beyond-one's-station Cinderella crap? That shit doesn't happen. They teach this crap to you in a place filled with rich assholes who don't give a damn about you. They want stupid sluts like me to fall for their crap when they will never, ever care about us. Never. Jane Austen sucks. Rich assholes who play their guitar and tell you they think you're "special" suck.

And Saint fucking Dymphna sucks.

Could I run away? Live off my wits. I picture it for a second. Me out there in the world living off my excellent talents in Latin and literature.

No. Too stupid. I am too fucking stupid.

Knock knock knock.

"Hey. You ok in there?"

It's the waitress.

"Yeah. Sorry. Um, bad cramps."

"You need a maxipad or something?"

"No, no. I'm ok. I'll be ok."

"Well, your dad is about three minutes from having a heart attack. You coming out?"

"Yeah. I'm sorry. I'm coming."

I stand. Wash my hands. Wipe my face. Flush the toilet to back-up my menstrual fib. Open the door.

I sit down to dry toast.

"Jesus, can't a girl crap without you calling in the National Guard," I say.

Dutch hasn't eaten any more of his breakfast since I left.

I take a bite out of the toast and nod to the waitress who looks less like she wants to spit than before. She smiles back but her pencil-brow topped eyes carry a whole bunch of…what? Pity? Maybe. That's ok. I could use some pity now. *Misericordia* means goodness inside. Unlike the word *Miseriae*. I am all full of *Miseriae* right now. But you can't see it. I am like the two-faced Janus. Only more of an asshole.

Dutch is eating his food again. "So Saint D's a good place. It's not like in the movies. You'll see. And you know, they got a lot of woods around there and stuff. I know you like the woods. Jesus…." He looks at me a long time. "Look, if that boy did something, I can make it right, ok? I mean, he didn't…do something…you know…."

Wow, this is hard for him. I am trying to figure out what exactly is the worst thing that is in his mind now. Did Schuy screw me? Absolutely. Did he take my virginity? Yep. Did he wear white after Labor Day? Probably not. Oh wait. He plays squash, so….

Then, I think I get it. Dutch is afraid that Schuy raped me. I don't know. How do you reconcile the fact that the man who sleeps with your mom is worried about your sex life? It's creepy, and I don't know how to deal with it. I mean, what does he expect me to say? He can't even buy tampons at the supermarket without turning beet-red. Does he want details? Highlights? What exactly does he think he'll do when he can't even make eye contact with Schuy's father?

"I just hate him," I say, knowing it's a lie. Because I don't hate Schuyler. I love him so much it hurts. I just want that stupid preppy asshole to love me back. And he doesn't. "He's a creep."

"You doing drugs? I know a lot of kids in your school do."

"Couldn't afford it even if I wanted to."

Dutch sighs and shakes his head, "Always a joke with you."

"He broke my heart." Don't know why I said that. Just came out. It's the first honest thing I've said since crushing Schuy's guitar and using Aquanet and his shitty Smiths-wannabe song notebook to light it on fire.

Dutch looks like maybe, just a little, he doesn't really hate me.

"Kid, I'm sorry." He shakes his head. "You know, this place you're going, it's just a way to keep you out of trouble. We'll find a good school when this is over. Your mom misses the hell out of you. It'll be good to have you back home. This place won't be easy, but…it's not jail."

"He told me to call him."

Dutch sighs and takes another bite of food. "Guys like that…." He shakes his head. "They…." But he had said all there was to say.

Guys like that.

Don't fall in love with girls like me.

"I won't call him. I promise."

"I'm gonna believe you." He finishes his food. I wrap my toast in a napkin and put it in my pocket.

Back on the road, I roll the window all the way down and Dutch doesn't complain. We talk a little about what's going to happen after high school's over. We don't mention working out my "crazy" in Saint Dymphna's or anything, just that it will be over, and I'll go on.

I tell him I want to go to college in New York. Maybe the New School. He thinks that's nice.

I start crying when we pass the exit to Springfield.

My stepfather lets me cry.

I won't call Schuyler.

I won't.

People fall in love and fall out again.

People go a little crazy.

People start again.

People forget what it feels like to lie beneath the trees listening to someone else breathe.

People forget these things and go to the New School. Or Columbia. Or NYU. Or just go to a place where people like Schuyler and his asshole father are just as small as everyone else.

All I had to do was hold it together for a little bit. All I had to do was follow the rules.

"You know, there's this new show on Broadway called 'Phantom of the Opera.' How about you, me, and your mom go when you get out of this place? Supposed to be real good. Plus I know an Irish restaurant near Times Square that's got great food."

"Great Irish food? Isn't that an oxymoron?" My tears have turned to sniffles.

"Always the jokes with you."

I allow myself a little more time to cry. To think of the thing that made me feel as if I might shatter. I'd give myself time. Maybe till I saw signs for Albany. Then, I'd be ready. Ready to let love burn up like his guitar. I'd see the signs and stop thinking of Schuy.

I see the sign.

No. I'll stop when we get closer to Plattsburgh.

I need more time.
But I will stop.
I will.
When we reach the city.

"Jane Austen Sucks"

A.M. METIVIER is a French-Canadian African-American writer and editor, living in New England, in the United States. She is "old enough to remember Commodore computers," and uses initials in her pen name because her full name is destined to be mispronounced everywhere outside of the province of Quebec. Her work has been published in the *Writer's Digest 13th Annual Short Short Story Competition Collection* and in *Mrs. Shushman Says Goodbye* (a short story collection).

She says: "Bradbury's first and last lines in this year's competition conjured a journey, and I remembered a seven hour trip to Maine in a 1976 Plymouth Volare Sedan, curled up on the bench backseat with my blanket and pillows. In fact, I did that trip every year of my young life. I remember the 80s in that car well. Required reading lists with characters named Elizabeth Bennet, Juliet Capulet, and Hester Prynne. Kate Bush keening *Wuthering...Wuthering...Wuthering Heights!* on my Walkman. Ah, the smell of Raleigh cigarettes and cinnamon gum."

Rachel Salhi

Control Measures

IT WAS A PLEASURE TO BURN the fields of alfalfa, the wheat, barley, and oats that once fed livestock. Meat was a thing of the past, at least for humans. No one needed to harvest animal feed ever again. In a way, that knowledge was liberating.

Also, I couldn't let this farm fall into the wrong hands.

"Torch it," my training told me. I lit three matches, flicked them between the rows of ripening grain. My makeshift kindling—alcohol wipes and gauze pads—caught immediately.

I waited until the fields took, really took, with nearly-red flames and billows of black smoke. There was no saving it now.

The firefighters had to try anyway. I stared at the blaze until their screaming sirens forced me back into my rental car. They wouldn't understand this was necessary. That food as we knew it was over.

The High Desert writhing orange and black around me, I slipped away and headed south.

I don't usually take control measures, but state and local health officials are unavailable. Doubled over with flu-like symptoms, as is most of Southern California. Alpha-gal allergic reaction includes vomiting, fever, vomiting, hives, vomiting, and joint aches. Did I mention the vomiting? I'm still trying to get the stench of other people's bile out of my nose.

145

I spent last week playing disease detective for the CDC. Alpha-gal allergy—aka the meat allergy—wasn't new, but it had never been seen on this scale before, or this far west. The CDC dispatched boots on the ground to find cases and generate hypotheses about likely sources.

My team traced the California outbreak to *Amblyomma americanum*, the Lone Star tick, whose population exploded after a warm, wet winter in Colorado and Texas. We determined that birds and rodents carried the larvae to California, and white-tailed deer brought the adults.

But that's not all we found.

My rental has satellite radio. I tune into NPR and catch my boss' voice trailing off.

Damn it, I just missed the CDC's statement.

But the news host, Mary Frances, has follow-up questions. "For those of you just joining us, we're speaking with CDC Incident Commander Robert McGowan. Dr. McGowan, what caused the outbreak?"

"*A. americanum* is opportunistic," my boss says. "The tick will attach itself to humans whenever conditions allow. And in Southern California, that's often, especially over Fourth of July weekend."

"Right," Mary Frances says. "When people are at a barbeque or fireworks display, they're not thinking about their exposed ankles or arms."

"Exactly."

He's trying to calm her, you can hear it in his voice. Deliberate. Smooth and measured.

And he's holding back. It isn't just California or the usual 10 percent of certain populations we're talking about. We're seeing alpha-gal in upwards of 75 percent of *all* populations, and reports are still coming in from the Pacific Northwest, the Midwest, and the Eastern Seaboard.

Americans weren't the only ones who enjoyed the

holiday weekend: *A. americanum* feasted, too.

"In most of the cases we documented, the person never realized they'd been bitten," McGowan says. "However, the tick left a tell-tale sugar molecule in the host's bloodstream: Galactose-alpha-1,3-galactose. Alpha-gal for short."

Mary Frances keeps probing. "And now we have to avoid all meat?"

"Just red meat." McGowan pauses, like he's trying to slow her pulse with words alone. "Triggers include beef, pork, and lamb. Most meat animals carry alpha-gal. Primates, including humans, don't, so when we get bitten by a tick carrying alpha-gal, our immune system develops antibodies to fight off the molecule. Three to six hours after consuming red meat, allergic reactions appear. Symptoms range from severe stomach cramps to anaphylaxis."

I cringe. Why slow-walk the truth? Mary Frances can handle it, and the public needs to hear it. All of it.

Tell her she's now allergic to dairy products and wool and gelatin. That even the *smell* of frying bacon will cramp her stomach. That the lanolin in her moisturizer will blister her skin. That gelatin-coated capsules could send her into shock.

Spell it out for her: tell her she needs to carry an EpiPen for the rest of her life.

But he doesn't. So Mary Frances sounds almost optimistic. "For those of you just joining us, Incident Commander Robert McGowan confirms that poultry and fish are still safe to eat."

No, they aren't. He hasn't read my team's updated report. He's leading you down a path that might get you killed.

The Antelope Valley Freeway is deserted, so I don't feel bad about using my phone while driving. I punch in McGowan's digits. He's not picking up.

Then I text my team. Redfield is the first to respond: no words, just a photo of a burning orchard. It looks like one of those "you-pick" operations in Leona Valley. Peaches and nectarines, plums and pears, a few cherry trees.

My hands are shaking. Is it low blood sugar? When was the last time I ate? A day ago, two?

I try to remember when my symptoms appeared. When did I first notice the fever?

I blast the air conditioner and push away the thought of peaches, their sweet, golden flesh.

Jesus I miss food.

The blare of firetrucks pulls me out of the moment. I catch two trucks in the rearview mirror. Where the hell did they come from, and how did they find enough firefighters to operate them?

I'm the only car on the road, but I make room. As the firetrucks roar past I realize I must be close to Redfield's blaze.

"When you're finished here," I text him, "head to Santa Monica Pier."

"?"

"Not to burn, to eat. Tell Arias."

Mary Frances is taking calls now. Public reaction ranges from confusion to anger to relief.

"It's like Nature itself wants humanity to kick the meat habit," says a PETA activist named Donald.

Meat eaters call in to debate the suffering of farm animals, while others question their spiritual beliefs. "If God is punishing us for animal abuse, why didn't He spare those who ate organic, free-range meat?"

Then the environmentalists pile on, and the crosstalk descends into chaos.

"The death of the meat industry is a good thing," insists a caller named Kate. "It will reduce the environmental impact on the planet. It takes 2,400 gallons of water to produce a pound of meat, and only 25 gallons for a pound of wheat."

Kate has a point, but now isn't the time to make it.

What she doesn't know is that plant-based foods are about to become a thing of the past, too. What no one outside my team knows yet is that we aren't just dealing with an outbreak but also evolution.

I text Ikeda, "How's the report coming?"

"First draft done. Want to look it over?"

"No time," I reply. "Email directly to McGowan, then head to Santa Monica Pier."

Somewhere along the 5 Freeway the cramps kick in. I toss my phone into the passenger seat and grip the wheel with both hands.

"Hey, Siri," I say between clenched teeth, "do I have any new voicemail?"

"You have three new voicemails," chirps the virtual assistant.

"Call Dr. Audie Shaw on speaker."

The ringtone thunders through the car's sound system, then comes my mother's "leave a message" spiel.

I try not to sound too desperate. "Hi, Mom. It's Bria. Hope you and Dad are enjoying Rome."

I choose my next words carefully.

"Listen, I've got a situation, and I could use your professional opinion. You know *Ideonella sakaiensis*? That new plastic-eating bacterium discovered in a recycling center in Japan? You're a teaching university, so I'm betting you've at least read about it. Anyway, I have a case where the bacteria are taking over a patient's gut. If you were the gastroenterologist on call, what would you do?"

I want to end the call there, but I can't. Maybe it's the

fever baking my brain.

I ramble.

"It's possible microbiologists could have detected *I. sakaiensis* in humans sooner, but I guess no one thought to look there, right? And in our defense, human gut flora consist of *trillions* of bacteria. My team only stumbled across it while investigating the alpha-gal outbreak."

My intestines clench so hard I practically growl.

"Sorry about that. Where was I? Oh yeah. Strictly speaking, *I. sakaiensis* is a 'beneficial' bacterium. Think of all the plastic-wrapped sandwiches we've eaten, all the water bottles we've held to our lips. *I. sakaiensis* helped us break down all those ingested microplastics. Yay."

I can't stop and her mailbox won't cut me off.

"The problem is, *I. sakaiensis* is now dominating and displacing all other intestinal flora. Picture Homo sapiens displacing Neanderthals. It's like that. In my gut. Right now."

Shit. Did I just give myself up?

"My team documented it in every case we've seen. The effect is most pronounced in those recovering from alpha-gal infection, but it's also present in those who've tested negative for alpha-gal."

Then it occurs to me this may be the last message I ever leave her.

"In short, bacteria is turning me into a plastivore. The good news is, I'll have a ubiquitous food supply. Plastic covers the entire Earth, right? The bad news is, in a few hours I won't be able to digest anything else. Just plastic. Okay. Hopefully you guys are unaffected in Rome. Love to Dad."

The cramps have subsided, but now I can't take my eyes off the water bottle in the cup holder.

I'm on the 405 Freeway when McGowan finally answers. He reads my team's report, but it's not the reaction I expected.

"Your conclusion is bacteria and evolution?" I can almost hear him shaking his head. "We'll hold off on another statement until we have more documented cases."

"You mean more fatalities."

"At this point it's correlation and not causation."

"With respect, sir, we're not the FDA. Our duty is to alert—"

The call ends. When I call back, I go straight to his voicemail.

The bastard hung up on me.

My hands quaking with anger and hunger, I text Ikeda. "Email the report to the press."

She's too quick to reply. "No can do. McGowan just called."

I park in the middle of the 405, then empty my water bottle onto the oil-stained asphalt. I work my fingernails under the bottle's paper label, slowly peeling it off.

I press my tongue against the bottle, halfway between the neck and body. Slowly I rotate the bottle like an ice cream cone, leaving it slick with saliva. The clear plastic softens under my tongue. The flavor is slightly sweet. Have I never noticed before? Or is *I. sakaiensis* now in my saliva, too?

This is going to take some getting used to.

My stomach growls and I take the entire bottle top— neck, threads, and all—between my teeth. I bite down, but the sound isn't the crinkle and crush I expect. It's more of a crunch, like potato chips, but the texture quickly turns to taffy. I try to chew but the mass sticks to my molars, nearly gluing my jaw shut.

I'm about to pull the plastic from my teeth when my

mouth waters and the mass slides effortlessly down my throat.

I meet my team—or what's left of it—on Santa Monica beach. Ikeda is a no-show, but Redfield and Arias wear the same weary expression and reek of smoke, of counter measures.

"You hit the urban centers?"

Arias nods. "Burned the chain stores. The Costcos and Whole Foods. Got that huge one on Arroyo Parkway."

I tap my temple. "It looks like you got your eyebrows, too."

He shrugs. "Didn't know how flammable alcohol wipes were until today."

The sun sinks, taking the tide with it. Left behind are pockets of seaweed and food wrappers, seashells and drink bottles. Grocery bags stretch the length of the beach, then disappear into the horizon. But instead of the usual disgust, all I feel is hunger. I swear I can smell the plastic, just a hint of sweetness. Like a fat yellow peach.

Redfield squats, plucks a bottle cap from a gritty pile of salt- and sand-crusted litter. He pops the cap into his mouth, his eyes darting as his jaw works the plastic. "Definitely better with salt. Almost like a cashew."

I claim a grocery bag while Arias jabs a straw into his mouth like a licorice stick.

We make a show of chewing so no one has to speak. But we all sense it: the possibility we'll be the only three people to survive this collision of evolution and bureaucracy.

Finally Redfield breaks the silence.

"There's a radio station studio a couple miles west." He points in the direction of street lights flickering to life. "We could give our own statement. Who wants to go on live radio?"

Arias shrugs and then turns to me. "I'd freeze up. Can

you wing it?"

I'm still pulling at the grocery bag with my incisors; the plastic stretches but doesn't tear. "I've been winging it all day."

Redfield stoops for another bottle cap. "Great. I'll text the station manager when we reach the city."

"Control Measures"

RACHEL SALHI is a content manager in California, in the United States. She likes to do most of her brainstorming while training for and (slowly) running ultramarathons. "Control Measures" is her first published short story.

She says: "This story took two weeks and 26 drafts. I tapped into my own fear of suddenly developing a meat allergy and not being able to eat my favorite foods. I also wanted to explore how a bigger food calamity might play out. A planet full of plastivores would benefit the environment, but could we adapt to the change? Would we even want to?"

Christopher Rowson

The Beginner's Guide to Endings

IT WAS A PLEASURE TO BURN. A simple singular thrill. Watching the heavy grate sink into the blaze, seeing the dashboards twinkle. Lenka caught it from time to time through her mask: that dizzying chemical spike. Melted plastics and liquified metals. Rubber, fabrics and glass. Sometimes, the cage would return with something still inside: an ashy blackened lump. And into the flames it would go once again. The residue of lost, unclaimed, unsellable things. Things that had attained a unique level of unwantedness: single odd socks and shoes, dirty underwear, unclaimed keys, assorted sex toys and drug paraphernalia, items deemed so offensive to conventional taste that they were wrapped and sealed before arrival—all of it, caged and dunked, disappearing into the smoky churning drum of the incinerator.

Lenka hadn't always worked in the hotel burn room. For a year or so she'd worked upstairs in the pink-tinted light of the Lost Property Department. She'd been a sorter, a logger of loss. She labelled items in the hotel computer system, gave them a description, put them in the box ready for storage. If no one claimed their property after sixty days it was removed. Some items, items of value, would be sent off to auctions—the watches and the jewelry, the silk scarves and the designer bags. The cheaper things were given away to charities and schools (when did those words start sitting comfortably in a sentence together?). Anything that couldn't be sold or gifted was sent clattering down an enormous aluminum chute that opened out into the burn room below.

"Hell," someone had answered when Lenka asked where the chute went. "Dark, hot, full of bastards." It wasn't until she went down there herself to retrieve a hat (her plumb-coloured beanie snatched and sent chuteward) that she realised what she was missing. It was far and away the most beautiful thing she'd ever seen. There was something of the Revelation about it. Real lake of fire stuff. She watched through grotty spare goggles as a gaudy plastic candelabra vanished with a hiss, never to grace tasteless table spreads again. And she was hooked.

A week later she was donning the goggles once more, putting her hasty training into practice. Pulling her PVC gloves over the exposed parts of her wrists. Remembering to close the cage fast. Remembering, lest the workers of the burn room tease her, to use the term *unclaimed* property rather than lost. The distinction was important, it seemed. Important in the way that going back for things you've left behind is important. Things that might have, at the time, slipped your mind. But let those upstairs concern themselves with value. Down in the basement the only game was erasure. Everything that came rattling down that silver chute went into the flames, into the lake of fire.

Lenka realised that the stuff in the burn room was as unwanted as it was substantive. It was often more personal than the items that stayed upstairs—those things could belong to anyone. They were being repurposed. Reprieved for continued use. But here, in the stifling burn room of the Royal Battersea Hotel, the items often contained something of their owners. There were, for instance, bags upon bags of what hotel management like to call 'electronic peripherals': SIM cards for phones, memory cards for cameras, hard-drives torn from laptops and computers. The shells of these items were left upstairs, the guts were sent below. Yes, Lenka had let curiosity get the better of her a few times. She'd burned a few empty packets. Took a few things home. But what was unclaimed was unwanted. And what was unwanted, she felt, was free.

She started small. A couple of USB sticks and one of those old portable hard drives that you could plug in. She had some fairly clear ideas of what she hoped to find, a sort of snooper's Bingo. Mainly what she wanted was evidence. Evidence of an affair, or some other kind of human failing. Of a crime perhaps, maybe just a light one—fly tipping locations or something. Light tax evasion (can it ever be light?). Maybe evidence of a secret family kept in regular payments and child support. Evidence of a secret habit. She wondered if the person who had failed to claim their property might be famous. A politician or a celebrity chef. She wondered if she might find content that newspapers would pay good money for. Some salacious or compromising material.

She tied back her hair, unzipped her bag on the kitchen table and took out her phone. Missed call. She didn't need to look to know that it would be Madeline. She put the phone screen-side down on the table and reached for the first USB stick.

Only now, waiting for the little device to initialise did she remember the stories of infections, of contamination. Organisational infrastructure brought down by certain executable programs that lurked within. Ready to spread. Vicious malware or viruses that take weeks to clean. Boring-looking files called webdat.dll or tenalec_win.exe. She thought of the end that had been set for this piece of plastic and metal. She thought of the tiny circuit board inside, melting away in the fire. She wondered how robust these memory sticks were, how much it would need to melt before it was rendered useless. She wondered why, sometimes, these things were called keys.

A window with several folders appeared on the screen, one of them intriguingly titled 'Constants.' She began to click through, wishing that she'd had the foresight to pick up some wine on her way back home. There were a few photos of a young woman with auburn hair eating a hotdog in what appeared to be Times Square. There were a few PDF documents about soil erosion and plastic contamination of the seas around the Mediterranean. And there were a few spreadsheets. One of them, Lenka was surprised to find, contained thousands of names and email addresses. She was unsettled. It felt like snooping around someone's kitchen only to find that it opened out into acres of garden. What could you call that? Data within data? A data trove? Oddly, this unsettled her more than the prospect of finding something dark or dangerous.

She was almost relieved when the second USB stick contained nothing but a couple of pirated children's movies and a recipe for pumpkin risotto. The portable hard drive, covered in colourful stickers—nuclear symbols, red lips, fiery skulls and the like—refused to start. Lenka usually persevered with these things. Unplugged and re-plugged. Checked the cables for wear. But she set it aside instead. She'd take it back, along with the USB sticks, and burn them, as she'd been paid to do. As had been originally intended for them.

In the weeks that followed, Lenka settled back into her work. She respected the rules to the letter, did as she was told. Everything that came down to the basement went into the flames. Nothing was slipped into that funny pocket in her bag that you had look really hard to find. She was a model employee. She still took great pleasure in burning, even taking on some extra shifts at the weekends. But still, she felt a little wince in her heart each time a bag of flash drives or memory cards tumbled from the chute.

On Easter Sunday, on a train rattling west out of the city, she phoned Madeline. They spoke of nothing much for a while. When there was a lull in the conversation she wanted to tell her she missed her. She wanted to say she forgave her. But she didn't. What she said was this: "I found out last week what happens to the ash! It gets sent in big drums to Amsterdam and used for some kind of flood wall ...."

Two-hundred burns in three days. The burn room like a furnace. Burners going up to the surface for gulps of fresh air. All eyes on the chute for the next thing to melt. Lenka was the first to see it arrive. "I've got it," she found herself calling above the hum. The largest bag of electronic peripherals they'd had in a while. Lenka wondered if this was how beachcombers felt. She'd have to be quick. The bags were only supposed to be opened for a second or two. A cursory check for bulky items. She took her gloves off. Against protocol, but it helped with the sifting.

At home, she scooped the things she'd taken from the burn room out of her bag. The haul: six memory cards and four USB drives. All she could gather in a couple of swipes. She'd remembered the wine this time and went to the kitchen to open it. Sitting back down, glass in hand and giddy with anticipation, she tried a few. Some of them were password protected. One of them was empty. Others held lots of family pictures: chubby cheeks and ice cream, day breaks in Margate, little angels terrorising the family dog. She spread the rest out on the table like scattered dominos and picked out one that shone; oily blue-black like the colour of crow feathers. She inserted the device into her laptop and opened up its contents.

Just one file.

Lenka felt a little cheated. She'd envisaged something more bountiful. She looked again at the window open on her desktop, at the single file. A word document called, of all things, The Beginner's Guide to Endings.

She opened it and scrolled through what appeared to be pages and pages of photographs. Some of them crisp and clear, some of them hazy and speckled. Some of them looked old—they had that Sixties feel, that Polaroid teal and orange. On first glance some of them seemed to contain very little in the way of subjects or scenery, and the quality varied dramatically. Some of them looked like amateur smartphone snaps. Others looked as though they'd been taken from news websites or captured from old newspapers.

She scrolled back up to the top of the document and looked at the first image: a black and white photo of a man standing on a train platform, hands in the pockets of a long trench coat, his head slightly bowed. Lenka tried to zoom in on the man's face but the low-resolution image yielded only snow. She scrolled to the next one. This one was much more vivid. It was a picture of magnified bacteria, a microscope shot. The image seethed with purple and red, each gloopy blob ringed by a bristly black skirt. The type of image that moves even though you know it's static. She'd seen something similar many times before, time-lapsed on TV, the blobs wobbling and quivering and touching each other though they looked like they didn't really want to.

She moved to the next image. A smiling man with a widow's peak and a fabric cap. Head up and out of a small window dotted with rivets, a single lean hand waving. It looked like the cockpit of some craft. And beneath him, painted in thick capital letters were the words ENOLA GAY. She opened a browser window and typed the words in, and then sat there for a least an hour reading about the plane. About the bombs, the cities, the destruction. Lenka even read about Mrs Enola Gay Tibbets herself, she of atomic bomb death-plane name fame.

Back to the document and ignoring her rumbling stomach. Lenka scrolled quickly through the next ones: a forest fire, credits rolling on an old television set, boarded up shops and an abandoned factory, chickens in a battery farm, a conductor bowing on a stage. There was something mollifying about the images. They affected a kind of newsreel stupor in her. Pages and pages of them, on and on. A woman standing with a little girl outside a hospital, the white cliffs of Dover, a crowd watching a building being demolished, two people sitting in a bar looking in opposite directions.

It was well past midnight before Lenka closed the lid of her laptop. She could see blocks of different colours rising when she closed her eyes. Like a film reel with scenes spliced and jumbled. She brushed her teeth and crawled into bed drunk and hungry and happy.

The following Saturday, Lenka stood by the ticket gates with her shoulders in, trying not to get bumped and shunted. She'd never seen the station this busy. When Madeline finally appeared looking flustered, Lenka gave her a wave and a stiff hug and they made their way out towards the taxis. While they waited in the queue, Lenka shifted the strap of her bag on her shoulder. Her laptop was old, and heavy.

"I've got something to show you," she said to Madeline. "Maybe later, though. When we reach the city."

"The Beginner's Guide to Endings"

CHRISTOPHER ROWSON is a UK writer who is taking a short break from his first novel to concentrate on short stories. When Christopher is not writing he is thinking about writing. And when he's not thinking about writing he spends his time reading, which makes him think about writing. A small amount of time is set aside for eating and battling house cats. "The Beginner's Guide to Endings" is his first published short story.

He says: "This story is definitely not based on my wife who is definitely not a serial snooper and is certainly not in possession of several salacious videos of strangers. This story asks how much our digital possessions are worth in a world of disposable content, and to what extent they are a true reflection of ourselves. Enjoy!"

Jessica Dealing

Cranes

IT WAS A PLEASURE TO BURN. Myra sat on the fire escape with her enormous neon green cast jutting out in front of her, and lit paper crane after paper crane with matches. Each one smoldered for just a second before long, thin tendrils of flame consumed it, a bird on fire. A phoenix, she thought as she watched, hypnotized, imagining the smoke dancing from the flame tip as the bird's new spirit. She felt like a phoenix too, lately, a fresh Myra ripping through the old Myra shell as if it was paper. She watched the crane curl and shrivel into a skeleton on the metal grating, until it turned to a jagged, powdery-soft ash.

Her teacher had personally delivered the paper cranes yesterday, a get-well project she must have assigned to Myra's class. Even though it took a thousand cranes, Myra knew, for the gods to grant you a wish, and she only had twenty-eight—there were twenty-eight others in her class— she was still touched that the other kids made the effort since she generally felt disliked, not just at school but everywhere. The gesture put her in such a good spirit, in fact, that she brought the box of folded cranes to Ms. Doris' house so she could admire them while she recovered enough to return to school. Ms. Doris was watching her during the day while her mom and dad were at work. Each crane had the name of the student who folded it written on a wing in pen. She picked up one of the paper birds and turned it slowly, adoring its angles. She unfolded it carefully, craving the histories in its creases, the secrets of its creation. When Myra finished opening the paper, she saw there were words inside. She flipped it right side up. "Myra you suck," it said.

Confused, she turned the paper over. Zachary's name was written on the other side, in the same handwriting. Jerk, she thought. He's the one who pushed her off the top of the slide to begin with. He's the reason her leg broke. *A clean break*, the doctor had told her mom. But it hadn't felt clean when she was lying face down in the dirt beneath the slide. Was there hate mail written in all the cranes, folded and hidden from their teacher? She wouldn't give them the satisfaction of reading any more of their messages.

There was a book of matches in the odds-and-ends drawer at Ms. Doris' which she allowed Myra to open whenever she needed something like scissors or a marker. So while Ms. Doris' piano student was over, Myra snatched the matchbook and the box of cranes and crawled out the guest bedroom, where she was often banished to play, and onto the forbidden fire escape outside, lugging her heavy, casted leg with her.

Now, sitting next to her on the metal landing, was a growing pile of ash. Myra liked to think that every crane she burned represented the student whose name was on the back, like small avian voodoo dolls. She imagined putting a curse on each of them as she lit the cranes, one after the other. The curses varied with each classmate. She cursed Billy with the uncontrollable urge to scream "poop head" at the least appropriate times. That was for cutting in line at the water fountain after gym class last week. She cursed Ella with malaria. That was for always making farty noises behind her in the hallways. She didn't know what kind of disease that was exactly, but she liked the way the word moved her tongue. Besides, any disease was too nice for Ella. She cursed Maria P. with wetting her pants, and Maria S. with bad B.O. The former told Zachary that Myra had cooties to begin with; the latter did nothing in particular, but she wore a hairbow with a crystal rose in the center that Myra coveted. And she especially cursed Zachary, with the worst thing she could think: warts. All over his body but a double layer covering his stupid, handsome face.

From the fire escape she could see over the apartment building's brown wooden fence, and beyond that the railroad tracks. Ms. Doris said the trains stopped coming long ago, but that didn't stop Myra from wishing for one to hop on and ride back to her house. She imagined herself on her way to the train tracks as a cartoon in this scenario, with her most precious possessions bundled in a rag and tied to the end of a stick that she'd carry over her shoulder. In this vision she wore overalls, though in fact she didn't own any and never had.

Lost in daydreams, she noticed the silence of the piano at the last minute, and hurried to open the window and scooch backward into the bedroom, minding her hindered leg. "Myra!"

Myra fell the short distance from the window to the floor and looked up from the carpeting where Ms. Doris' ridiculous gold house slippers glittered at her, to her hands on her hips, to her red-rouged frown, a monochromatic rainbow. All the creases on her face pointed in a downward direction, and Myra knew not only that she'd be in trouble, but that her mom would hear about it. "What are you doing? And what's burning? I smell fire." Myra quickly sat up and attempted to slam the window shut, but Ms. Doris shoved her out of the way and peered out, spotting the abandoned box of cranes and the matchbook. She turned from the window, fixing Myra with a terrible gaze. "Matches? Why? Why do you have matches? Answer me! What were you trying to do?"

Myra tried several times to answer but she didn't know to which question she should respond. And did Ms. Doris mean what she was trying to do, like on a physical level? Because wasn't the answer insultingly obvious, given the burned paper and the box of cranes? Or did she mean something else? Because how was she supposed to know that? Was she trying to weed out a deep-rooted feeling of rejection? Since she didn't know how to express all these thoughts, she sat there saying nothing, watching the floor.

Ms. Doris marched to the window, clapped it shut, and locked it for good measure, as if this wasn't the way Myra'd gotten out in the first place. "You stay right there. Your mother is going to know about this." Ms. Doris glared at her, then added, "*Missy.*" She stormed out of the room, but not before regarding her one last time with what Myra thought of as a bug stare. As if Myra was an ugly cockroach she squashed with a rolled-up magazine, only to find its guts all over her clean carpet.

Myra could hear her walk down the hallway, speaking into her cell phone. Myra inched closer to the doorway of the room and eavesdropped. Ms. Doris' voice was hard to hear, almost just a loud whisper, and Myra only caught pieces. She heard Ms. Doris ask her mom what was wrong with her, and say that she should have come with a warning. Then something about making a right decision. She ducked back from the door when she heard footsteps approaching. Ms. Doris muttered, "Thank God it's not official yet," and walked past Myra, down the hall to her own room. The conversation—the parts she could hear, at least—made her uncomfortable. She didn't like to be talked about. It made her feel like a freak. She sometimes thought everyone was psychic except her, like they could see something about her that she couldn't.

Ms. Doris charged back into the room, intruding on Myra's thoughts. "*You,*" she said, "are going to sit right there and not move until your mother gets here." Then she marched to the heavy bureau that held her "winter clothes" and tried to move it over a few feet to block the window. Myra watched, mildly smug, as Ms. Doris managed to budge the monstrosity into place but not without grunting and breaking a sweat. "I'm locking this door so you can't do any more damage." Ms. Doris slammed the bedroom door shut and Myra heard the click of the lock. The glowing red alarm clock on the nightstand read 4:00. Her mom would be here around 5:30. Myra sighed.

The main problem was this wasn't the first time she was caught with fire. A couple weeks ago she had taken her mom's lighter from the end table next to the couch and she was trying to flick it like her mom did, who used a lighter because she smoked cigarettes, even though she told Myra not to say anything about it to her dad. Myra was only trying to copy her, the easy careless way she made flame appear from her own hand, like a god, Myra thought. Like having superpowers. Myra still couldn't make it do anything but spark when her mom had stepped into the room. Her mom asked what she was doing, and Myra was too embarrassed to say she was trying to be like her, because how could Myra ever really be like the beautiful woman who stood before her. She'd only be insulting her. Her mom had spent the rest of the evening—until her dad got home from work—acting strange. Like she was afraid of her.

Myra sobbed into a teddy bear that leaned gently on a stack of pillows. And now Ms. Doris was going to tell her she was playing with matches. Her mom would think she was a freak just like everyone else and there was nothing she could do about it.

She knew, really, that her parents found out the truth that day, that the principal probably told them. She had pushed the boy first. Zachary. She didn't confess because it made her look like the bully when, really, she was the victim! And anyway, she pushed him because he called her shirt ugly, the purple one with ruffles her mom bought for her before the school year started. Zachary was the one who started it. And she was so sick of kids being mean to her. Earlier that day, Maria P. said she had cooties and so Myra was already in a bad mood when Zachary insulted her shirt. After that she *had* to show them they couldn't mess with her. She waited till the recess monitor was on the other side of the playground and went over to where Zachary was standing, last in line on the third rung up the slide. Myra ran over, pushing him from it at top speed. Zachary fell from the ladder. He only got the wind knocked out of him and came to quickly—just after Will ran off to tattle on her.

Her mother entered the room as Myra wiped the last of her tears, and immediately her heart raced. She anticipated her mom would be angry or worse but instead she knelt over her. "Are you ready to go?" she asked softly.

Her mom thanked Ms. Doris on their way out, told her she'd call her later and keep her *informed*. Ms. Doris nodded. Myra avoided Ms. Doris' gaze as she hobbled after her mom on her crutches, her armpits aching. In the car a distant anxiety gnawed at her, of the time before. But *this* was the beginning, she told herself, forcing a smile.

"Why are you smiling, honey?" her mom asked. There was something different in her voice that Myra didn't like. Her tone took on an edge, devoid of the soft voice she'd just used inside.

"Are you okay?" Myra asked.

They were driving slowly, steadily, on the main road connecting Ms. Doris' street with their own. Her mom sighed like she was trying to summon the energy to act sweetly. "I'm fine." But she glanced at her funny, like Myra was a math problem she couldn't solve. When she didn't say anything else, Myra turned her attention to the passenger window.

She knew the turns now. The way back home. There: the familiar oak that grew closer to the street than any other tree. And there: the crack in the curb, and she knew next they'd reach the stop sign. Tonight after dinner Myra would suggest playing Chutes and Ladders with her parents, and they would all sit on the living room carpet, playing and laughing, just like that first week. She would find a way back to that first week. There: her street.

Then it passed. Myra turned in her seat to watch their stop sign fade to background. She swallowed. "Where are we going?"

Her mom reached into her purse and brought out a

cigarette and her lighter. She didn't answer until she pulled from it a long drag, and Myra thought she looked like a dragon when she blew the smoke slowly out the open window. "We're going to the city, honey."

Myra's stomach backflipped. They had no reason to go back there. It was where she was from. "Why?"

Why else? a voice from inside her seemed to say. But no, she wouldn't do that, Myra argued internally, not mom. Or even dad. And they were her parents. They told her so. Months ago. That first week they told her. Call us Mom and Dad. Parents didn't just return their kids.

She didn't have a thousand cranes. She didn't have enough to buy a wish from the gods, but maybe they'd listen anyway. *Please!* she screamed in her head. *Please don't send me back there.*

Her mom smoked a second cigarette and smiled at her, and Myra wanted to claw the smile from her face because it didn't match her eyes. Her eyes were somewhere else, far away, dreaming of someplace Myra was not. "Mom," Myra said in a small voice.

"Hmm?"

"Maybe. . . we can go get ice cream later?"

"Ice cream?" Her mom repeated, still distant. There wouldn't be a later, but the lie was a balm, Myra hoped, for both of them. "Sure, honey. When we reach the city."

"Cranes"

JESSICA DEALING is a writer from Florida, in the United States. She likes eating cheese, drinking tea, and finding strange things to watch on Netflix. She's had her work published in *SmokeLong Quarterly*, *The MacGuffin*, and the *Manzano Mountain Review*.

She says: "Ah, to be a kid. With all the romanticizing we do about childhood, I think it's easy to forget how difficult it can be to navigate the world of adults. In this story I wanted to capture how at-odds a strong-willed imaginative child can be in the world. Myra turned out to be an interesting mix of myself and my mom who, from her childhood stories, sounds like she might have unknowingly been the neighborhood bully. (But I'm *almost* positive she was just very misunderstood!)"

Robert Lloyd Richardson

Riding the Bull
to the Louisville Market

IT WAS A PLEASURE TO BURN the entirety of the woodpile, of course, all the oak cut to length and split down to neatness. A pleasure, too, burning the woodshed piece by piece and then the shed proper, where the 1987 Olds Delta 88 had been parked since 1991. Now the Old Panda Mare is parked on the street.

And then the deeper thrill was burning the house itself, or the bones of it that could in fact be separated and cut to stove lengths. Simple conversion to heat, smoke, and embers, piece by piece. There was something akin to salvation in the act, cracking apart the old boards with my crowbar, picking the nails from the ash I'd shoveled from the cold stove in the morning. I have a tin can sitting on the flagstones alongside the Morning Glory that has at least fifty nails in it, most of them the old, forged and hand-cut kind, because the house dates to the 1890s.

The house, being tiny, heats easily from the one stove, the flame in a good draw beating a snare percussion four-time. There's a furnace in the basement crawlspace, but I haven't wanted to use it. We've been eating canned beans and frozen broccoli florets, cooked atop the woodstove. I am reverting to a simple, scrubbed-down life.

Burning everything. Somehow it became a project for me, goaded on as I was by the boxes upon boxes of family photos. I would say, "Mom, you want to look at photos?" and she would wave her hands to shoo even the mere possibility away. There were just too many, from the late Fifties onward, national park vacations and pet dog domesticity, with a special detour for my father's photography of huts and handshakes in Vietnam.

The first fistful of photos to be consigned to the flames were taken at my grandmother's house—my mother's childhood house—in the rural nowhere a few miles out of town. She'd grown up in just another hollow in the woods, a 'turn right at the old cider press' sort of place. Picture after picture of happy faces, the corners of their eyes hinting at despair or perhaps just the blinding summer sun.

A very old picture: my aunt's grandfather Ezra as a boy, seated on a bull cow. The tether trails down from the giant animal's halter to Ezra's older brother Michael, who might be as old as fifteen. Ezra would ride atop the bull the several miles it took them to get to market days in Louisville, such was the tameness of the bull and their skill with it. In my imagining of it, Michael is always asking why he doesn't get to take a turn on the bull as they make their way to the market.

"I'll tell you," Ezra says, "when we reach the city."

They burned with chemical alacrity. They did not, however, burn to nothing, instead leaving the oil-black char-sheen of the negation of paper, black scrim mounting up to more debris than you'd expect, so photographs are more of a project than, say, hardwood elephants from a trip to Africa in the Eighties. The wooden animals, spoons, and bookends burn to the finest imaginable ash.

I suppose I'm faced with the concern that Mother will outlive the wood supply, insofar as I can't take down the kitchen or her bedroom without her knowing, or knowing at least in that vague way that she knows things now. I drive into town to fetch canned meat and the white bread my mother favors, see the firewood outside the grocery alongside the big packaged ice box. I think, "firewood." But things aren't that far with burning the wallboards and I stick to foodstuffs, to deviled ham.

Back at home I check in. She's got the hospital bed that motors the top half of the bed to a slant, the bed delivered as part of a hospice program. She likes the monster grumbled up to position, from which she can spend the morning slowly sliding down into a puddle of bones at mid-bed. Her legs are stupid now, hardly ever listening, stiff like the wood I'm prying from the spare bedroom walls.

I say, "Well, don't you look comfortable."

"I doubt I look so very comfortable," she says. "But then I've been trying to see them all day."

"Who are you trying to see?" I ask, though I know she's gone to some unreal meeting in the relative distance and it's impossible to understand what anyone there says.

"Oh, I suppose you can't make them, not the way they've hardened themselves to things. But they surely, they, we need to convince them to pardon."

"Who's hardened?"

"No, just that it seems you can't turn to anyone anymore."

"Well, I wouldn't worry about them." I've gone to her, laced an arm under each shoulder, straining my back to lift her some small way up the incline. We'll do the complete reset at lunch. Such a fine bed to have in such an appalling matchbox-full of cheap deal dressers and chairs.

"Easier said than done," she says, meaning about not worrying.

"I suppose it is."

"Then there's the trouble of going off to meet them. I'm not as mobile as I'd like to be." She pats her hands in the general direction of her legs.

"No, I suppose not. But who are we going off to meet?"

"Well, I think it's just the ones who, you know, are making things happen. You see them out here, but really they come from the city. You think, how fast can you run from them? But here we are going to meet them."

"City people, then," I say.

"Yes."

"Louisvillians." Our destination, were we actually to have one, would be Louisville, across the fast swirl of the Ohio River from our lot on the Indiana side.

"Which is why I think we have to go and see them. Straighten things. Plus, the city, I know you enjoy it." She chuckles to suggest that my enjoyment is maybe not entirely on the up-and-up.

"What do I enjoy?"

"There's that theater on Main Street, and restaurants, I think you're fond of eating out."

It's possible that she's saying I'm fat, which I am. It's possible in equal measure that she simply means I have never been the country sort of person, which I'm not, which role she inhabits easily, like a possum its sleep.

The structure of the house lends itself to my purpose, the core of it built originally of logs, inside which there were later furring strips and, horizontally, plain wide boards, somehow never plastered, but instead painted white, with the lines of the boards showing through plainly. I imagine there are layers of lead paint under the current coat, and I don't care a whit about lead fumes.

Because these boards, along with various studs and joists from the sheds and the front porch, are long, I've set up a station on the porch where my dead father's chop saw reduces each to one-foot length.

Now she's saying: "I don't know what to do about my sister."

I don't know what to do with her sister, either, because her sister is dead. But she is referring to a dream or hallucination she had last night. Her sister had found some children wandering around outside and had, if I understood correctly, dispatched them with a pump-action shotgun.

Bloody as hell, if my mother's reaction is any indication.

My mother, tears streaming, says, "I don't know why she did that. And she's my sister; I don't want to call the police, but what do I do?"

She's at a terrible impasse and it's breaking her.

"I think you're mistaken, Mom. I don't think she actually did anything to the children." For the moment, this is tentatively accepted.

"Maybe I'm just confused, then."

"You see things at night that are confusing, you know," I say.

"What should I do then?"

"Maybe you want to watch some television?" I say.

"Turn it on, why don't you," and I nod, but I don't turn it on, because I know she doesn't mean it. If I turn it on she will cry and beg me to turn it off before the evil can take the house. I ask her about the television only because the question-and-response format seems to calm her.

"I'm going to the kitchen to work on dinner," I say.

"What's for tomorrow's dinner?" she wants to know.

"The remains of today's."

But instead of cooking I've gotten distracted and I'm burning more photographs. There is every permutation of every relation standing on every front porch and stoop that has ever figured in our family history. Her sister, the ostensible murderess, was perhaps my favorite relative. When I was a kid she was enough older that she was grown, sophisticated, wonderful. I find pictures of her and nine times out of ten she is with an equally beautiful girl cousin who lived in the house next door. Here they are in hula skirts.

I think of the pictures as lingering dreams of places and times that are gone, gone, except for a certain weight they leave behind in the image. This weight infinitesimal vanishes in the flames and, after two or three shoeboxes of pictures, the stove bathes me in a cheery hot sense of weightlessness that makes me feel reckless and alive.

I squint at a photo of this aunt, a photo made in the late Sixties. There's a series of these, all practically identical because my father would take photos at a gallop a half dozen in a stream on the theory that you could pick the best of them, the least of the eyes closing against the glare, then no one ever picked out the best of them and the whole series lived on forever in the shoebox. Here she's a young adult, trim white Peter Pan collar and a thousand buttons. Hair just so. This would have been when she was headed off for the city, first Louisville and then New York, but you can see in her eyes in these pictures, read it almost as if it were written in block letters, that she's too afraid. Too afraid to last. Too afraid to succeed.

You think you are living your life in such a way that you can see a progression, maybe as simple as farm, to village, to town, to city. It is as simple a progression as a thin album of photographs, featuring you, first with a dog, then a prom date, a spouse, a family, a sprawl of relatives on some occasion, everyone looking half dead, half smiling, standing on the porch. Why are there never photos of life around the posed moments, or pictures where you see yourself triumphant unto the day, your life possessed of meaning and sense?

"Will we go to the city?" my mother calls from the bedroom.

"Yes, I suppose we might," I call back, though I'm lying because I couldn't manage taking her to the city if I wanted to. We are marooned.

"We'll see a doctor, then?"

"We'll see whoever you need to, sweetie."

"I'd like to be back on my feet."

"Well, let's see what happens."

There's a picture of four generations of the family's women all together under a tree. Before that, not even pictures, just names on the overleaf of a family bible.

It sounds dramatic, I know, to burn the house from the inside out. A step back, though, and you see it's practical. What's needed is a good airing out and fresh application of modern drywall. It's a project I'm preparing for as I clean out the house and wait for my mother to die. Having burned all their death certificates, as my mother seems to have collected and saved them, I can tell you that previous generations didn't leave much of anything at all behind them and, as I'm the last man standing in the family, I know firsthand that these people aren't remembered. Moments they stood on porches on rural lanes are saved in black-and-white photos, but the names of most of them are lost. I burn the photos and the very question of their names is erased. I'll sell the place after the rehab.

After her afternoon nap, my mother wakes up strangely renewed. She stands up alongside the bed, the first time she has stood in weeks and I beg her to sit back down before she falls.

"Let's fire up the Old Mare Panda," she says, "and go for a spin."

"Where are you planning to go?" I ask.

"I'll tell you," she says, "when we reach the city."

"Riding the Bull to the Louisville Market"

ROBERT LLOYD RICHARDSON is an editor from Pennsylvania, in the United States. His most successful tactic for avoiding writing is to spend an incredible amount of time trying to build a credible folding electric guitar for travel. While many interesting things have occurred in his workshop over the years, a folding electric guitar that's worth playing isn't one of them. Still, he has no regrets. "Riding the Bull to the Louisville Market" is his first published short story, at least since college in the 80s.

He says: "This story is closer to home than I'd like. I wrote it while my mother was dying of Parkinson's Disease. For the record, I didn't burn her house down in small bits and pieces. But I did sort through a lot of her belongings, disposing of most of them. There was also a real bull ridden by real relatives to the market, but it was the Knoxville market. A photo was made for the *Knoxville Sentinel*; the boys look at ease."

Mariah Hopkins

Waiting for the Great Fire

"IT WAS A PLEASURE TO BURN," the hired pipsqueaks who started the fire promised. A troupe of boys so young they only had whispers of beard hair on their chins, they'd sprinted through the dark country hills to deliver word of their deed before we could even feel the heat of the blaze on our skin. Restless, we looked over the leafy gardens and cool pools of Caesar's provincial estate towards the black slopes where we knew Rome was fixed. The fire was still a light among lights, easily mistaken for any low star in the night, or lighthouse glowing warm for pulling sailors ashore. How long before the flame swelled large in the far-off hills? How long before smoke blacker than black boiled skyward to obliterate the soft darkness of our summer evening? We tittered amongst ourselves. The wine cups weighed heavy in our hands and all eyes moved slowly to Caesar Nero, belly-up and looking like a beached jellyfish on his dining couch. He contemplated the boys over the mound of his stomach, drink marred his pretty face with oily fatigue. Caesar clapped a hand against Poppaea's white leg, pushing on his wife's knee to raise himself upright.

"The arrangement was carried out as described I hope," Caesar snoozed, the freedman Sporus passing another drink into his hand.

The leader of the pipsqueaks stepped forward and we drank him up and down. He and his cohort were not what we were expecting of people bitter enough to kindle city-swallowing flames all over Rome. They were not street filth tantalized with coins and hot meals to do the emperor's bidding, but clean young men. All were healthy-skinned, bright-eyed, and spry with strong legs and expectant lips. They could have been our sons, nephews, or cousins. The leader was a beautiful Roman son, golden-haired and the closest to receiving his manly toga.

"Heaps of dry parchment were set aflame in spots around the Circus, Caesar," the leader said. We shivered at his voice, slick and confident. The purpose of Caesar's scheme was inherently good, good enough that we could press those who would be hurt by it to the back of our minds to be forgotten, but it was wicked for a child to not be troubled at all by his role in the misery.

"Heaps?" Poppaea repeated, snarling. Our heads snapped away from the child to her. The empress' cheeks were blooming red. "You were told not to leave any evidence of dirty work behind," Poppaea bristled, her towering wig of blonde curls trembling on top of her head.

The leader opened his mouth to speak but buttoned his lips together quickly. Caesar touched his wife's shoulder. "Calm, darling, the parchment will burn," he said to her. "Won't it, boy?"

The boy leader nodded vigorously. "All of the Caelian was burning by the time we left the city."

"Pity the flame is so small," Poppaea sneered, gesturing to the tiny fluttering light in the hills that was Rome. Caesar touched her shoulder again.

"Would you have the blaze reach Antium, love?"

Poppaea shifted uncomfortably in her seat, silent but not placated. Caesar swung his right arm open, whole body swaying with him. "Epaphroditus will pay your coin," he said, the boys following Caesar's direction towards his secretary. The dining patio was silent while the freedman doled out the pipsqueaks' money, the *shlink shlink shlink* of coins sliding against coins sounding in place of music. Impatient, Poppaea twirled her hand in the air and the band started to play again. Sleepy themselves, the musicians strung out a song that was low and long like an animal's bleat. Caesar lay down again, his wife's hand curling around his face as the music lulled him to sleep. We watched the boys skip away, purses jingling happily with new coin.

Like Caesar, some of us tilted our chins into our palms and fell asleep. Others trained their eyes back on the growing glint of light in the hills, unsure of what we were waiting for but aware that the rest of the evening rested on it. We were all brought to this dinner for one reason or another: Caesar considered us friends, we were distant cousins on his father's side, we were political confidants and artists he held dear. And whether we were all informed of Caesar's plan to sweep into a fire-ravaged Rome as a savior bringing alms of water and corn, or not, we were all pulled to Antium by the same fear of Caesar's fickleness. The boy who'd ten years ago come to the laurels with virtue and promise was gone, replaced by a capricious man cruel enough to cast his mother off into the mouth of the sea. An ignored invitation could be seen as treachery and after the death of the lady Agrippina there'd be no hesitation to lash at faithless friends, cousins, and confidants. We were drawn away from Rome with the promise that our homes would not be damaged. How could they be when the fire would be concentrated in poor areas? Areas where the people already had nothing and Caesar's rescue would be seen as more than it was. Yet we could not help but think about what we left behind in the city. Not only the apartment buildings we owned and our homes with family treasures inside, but the tiny restaurant by the circus we enjoyed, the manuscripts we'd left in the hands of copiers, the fawn statue by which we used to play as children, and the friends, parents, and siblings we could not warn.

We stared at that flickering light in the dark countryside for longer than the musicians could play, Caesar's secretary approaching them to say it was alright if they wished to retire. Those of us who were still awake slowly began to let our heads droop. Whatever we were waiting for had not yet arrived, but we knew it had when we woke in the morning to an orange tinged sky and the faint whiff of smoke.

We touched our heads, groggy and displeased by the nature of our wakeup call. Caesar was as wobbly as the rest of us, but Poppaea was awake and standing, arms crossed over a front stained by a dribble of vomit as she spoke in hushed tones to old Epaphroditus. Poppaea's curly wig dangled from her hand and, noticing her waking guests, she slapped it back on top of her head. It rested there lopsided and in need of some tending. We turned our heads towards the hills, no longer swathed in dark night and lush with the light of day. Fire ran along the rim of the hills in orderly lines, silent and harmless from so far away but close enough that a hint of hot smoke was in the air. Now that the fire was finally here we were uncertain of what to do. We rose from our seats and gathered at the edge of the patio, staring at it, talking amongst ourselves, sharing our disbelief. Last night the lot of us were so taken by the wine that the fire—Nero's plan—felt like a matter of course. Turn Rome into an inferno! Save the citizens from the devastation and look like a hero! But in the morning hours it was hard to believe that it was real: drunken schemes like this should never come to be.

Poppaea's clapping hands brought us to attention, we drifted away from the patio ledge and reassembled around her. Caesar was standing beside her now, still groggy but alert.

"Friends," Poppaea said, beckoning the last of us close. "As you've seen, the fire has grown in Rome. Messengers tell us that flames have crept through the streets, destroyed buildings, looters are breaking into homes and businesses."

Some of us clapped, unsure of how to take this news. It's what we were waiting for, but we couldn't help thinking about the businesses we owned and how much money Caesar's scheme would cost us.

"This is what we intended," Poppaea said. She addressed

the confused applause with her arms spread wide, palms up. The looting and destruction were things of benevolence. "Soon Caesar will return to Rome, ready to aid recovery efforts with coin, food, water, and clothes."

This statement definitely called for applause, all of us clapped and some thrust cups into the air. "Caesar, savior of Rome!" they shouted, Caesar blinking in response, the full weight of what was happening had not yet hit him.

"In four days we will leave for Rome," Poppaea continued. The cups in the air wilted. Four days? Why not now? Antium was not so far away, Caesar could be in Rome this afternoon if he wished it. We looked at one another, clueless dolts searching for answers. Did Caesar mean to cause the most destruction possible before taking action? We turned our eyes towards the emperor, swaying on spindly legs and rubbing his eyes. No, Caesar did not mean to destroy the city, but Poppaea did. Our stomachs churned as the air sickened with more smoke. It felt obvious and we were fools for missing it. The empress did not come by her position honestly, seducing Caesar and persuading him to divorce his first wife in favor of her. The head of Poppaea's rival was brought to her while she bathed, proof of her death. Rumors even existed that Poppaea was the one who organized Caesar's mother's death, since she didn't like the influence his mother held over her son. The collapsing boat and death at sea seemed too absurd to be believed until we felt the fire reach out to us, tickle our backs and bare arms with a dull lick of heat. Poppaea couldn't entirely ensure her safety as empress if her husband was acting erratically, turning himself into a fool for even the lowest laundry woman to see with his public poetry recitals. After everything she'd done to become his wife, organizing a great disaster to turn her husband into a hero of the people wasn't beyond Poppaea's capabilities.

"Uncertainty and fear will live in Rome no more," Poppaea continued, taking hold of her husband's shoulder and steadying him. "After the fire the people will see Caesar

Nero as the noble man we, his closest friends and family, know him to be." Caesar patted Poppaea's hand with his fingers. "And artist," she added, hastily. "They will finally know him as the true man and artist he is. Until then, we'll wait here," Poppaea said, trying to silence the doubts we were whispering to one another as her hair wiggled about on her head. "We'll wait in Antium until the fire is quenched and Caesar can travel without fear of the fire. He'll be a hero when we reach the city."

"Waiting for the Great Fire"

MARIAH HOPKINS is a recent graduate of the Vermont College of Fine Arts, in the United States. When not busy writing, she's a transfer advisor at the Community College of Rhode Island, and an administrative assistant at the YMCA. Her next big adventure? Going to Minneapolis to pursue video game journalism. "Waiting for the Great Fire" is her first published short story, but her work will also appear in an upcoming issue of *The Ocean State Review*.

She says: "I've been researching and writing about Ancient Rome since I was twelve, and I enjoy the challenge of meeting writing prompts with historical moments. The words *burn* and *city* made me think of the Great Fire of Rome, but I didn't want to perpetuate the myth of Nero fiddling while it burned. There are many theories as to why the troubled Nero might have set Rome ablaze. This is just one of them."

Katy Madgwick

Dust Jackets

IT WAS A PLEASURE TO BURN.

Or so the elders claimed, back when they had voices and stories and trod our paths before us. We nicknamed them "forgottens," and most of their stories have gone the same way. Most, but not all. Long years of darkness wound out behind us, the forgotten shadow of a road we travelled together. Now, varying degrees of night comprise a bleak palette of browns and greys, the "sun" a mere specter of a long-dead deity passed down as legend. The forgottens knew the sensation of heat from the heavens searing their skin pink, and they worshipped at its altar. We remember. *In memorium.*

Now there's just Iris, Killen and me. The only ones spared by this relentless tyrant season. Spared, or forgotten. We don't ask questions. The dust envelops us; we are half blind in its suffocating custody. And still we plough on. Stopping has always frightened Iris. Just the word— "stop"—with its round, clipped, bubble-burst suggestion of an ending haunts her wise blue eyes. An ending to what? Our journey? Our lives? Iris never explains.

Leader, mother or simply the tallest among us, we've forgotten why we follow her, but we do. And she won't let us say the "s" word, not ever. Let alone even think about trying it. So, when it comes time to rest, we hover instead, commas instead of full stops, sharing out scraps of vile subsistence and divvying up the patchwork of tasks peculiar to the fabric of our lives. Survival, and everything that entails.

We must have slept standing up. I can't recall a moment where I lay down, not fully. Maybe I rested my head on my own shoulder, my neck twisting so I could snuggle my cheek against something almost warm. I must have sat once, hunched over a fire, although I can't recall that either. Instead, my calves grow numb from crouching, always ready to run. Nowhere safe to sto—to pause.

Time is elastic these days, reams of the stuff thwart our progress. If only it wasn't so damn thick. Wading through time is worse than trekking up any hill. It's always there, viscous and unrelenting, sucking at your boots like some amorphous parasite. Not to mention the cold, of course. Rest invites a slow, creeping death, the clasping embrace of an insidious chill which threatens to possess you the second you let your guard down. So we face it head on. Wrapping our bodies like we do our faces, warding off evil in all its guises. Three mobile cocoons, shuffling inexorably along some preordained path like supplicant pilgrims. How long until we circle back and repeat it all? Will anything change?

Killen sees ghosts, he says. We stare blank as the night at him, searching long dead memories for the meaning of the word. Wondering how he knows it at his tender age. He means the dirt-gilded zombies who drift on unseen tangents drawn in the sand. They glide past in fossilized clusters, sometimes alone, not close enough to bother us; far enough to lack meaning to our vital band of three.

But Killen counts them compulsively; Iris and I try to forget the tallies he spouts daily. "Sixteen on the south ridge. Twelve to the West. Almost nineteen heading for the Reach."

"*Almost* nineteen?"

He shrinks into himself then, a shiver imperceptible as gossamer rippling across his face. Such a young face, yet it's etched with dust-dug pits, like the negative of braille.

Iris squeezes my hand sometimes, when the storms pick up and riffle the surface of the Earth, lifting sheets of dust like a theatre curtain. We might have seen the performance the remains of the planet had in store for us, were it not for the stinging gusts; plumes of dust raised, orchestrated, and delivered biting back into our faces. The crescendo comes at dusk, as whatever light filters in through so-called daylight hours gives up and slopes away, abandoning us to the gales of caustic particles. A guessing game of when and where and just how hard the next ones will land.

Iris squeezes my hand and I squeeze back, chin on my chest, face swathed in cotton, spit dry on my lips and nothing but arid stiffness left on my rusted tongue. Swallowing is a leviathan undertaking. No precious drops will reach our cracked lips until after the storm is done, unless we happen upon an upturned mountain to shelter behind. Human contact is hydration; fingers pulsing with the rare refreshment of it. Staying together is our single purpose; to allow any distance to creep between our bodies would mean surrendering to the sovereign dirt. Killen shielded behind, his head pressing into the small of my back as he reprises his role as the rear of a pantomime horse, for an audience of almost nineteen.

Day breaks with a damp snap after that, and we slow a little, gathering our senses. Killen's busy scanning the east horizon for ghosts when he asks: "What is that?"

We rub our eyes, questioning the evidence. Nudging through the layers of dust and gas that have strangled them all these long years, exhausted rays emerge. Is it a hallucination? Some collective dream? The sensation is something akin to divine reverie. Nirvana, the forgottens called it, a state of higher being. Literally higher, for Killen, his little legs dragging heavy steps up the nearest rise to the point closest to the heavens, as if in raising himself above us, he'll soak up the lion's share. I can't begrudge him this small victory, and witnessing anemic sunlight grace his pale forehead for the first time brings me to my knees. His smile so bright I fear for a moment it will scare the sun away. That seeing itself reflected in the almost transparent boy might send it scurrying back. None left for us poor wretches down at ground level.

Time snaps like an elastic band released, and instead of decades passing daily we count the precious, bejeweled seconds it takes for the rays to penetrate Killen's frail form and extend hope down to Iris and me. We lift our faces to welcome them and they stroke our dirt-caked cheeks and we laugh like we've been tickled.

The sunlight seeps through, spoon-feeding us molten joy. The sun was mourned by the forgottens like a lost relative, and her triumphant return exalts us. History loops back on itself as we connect to our ancestors, reclaiming what was lost to them. We are the chosen.

We don't burn at first, despite our translucent complexions, rendered paper-white through years of lack. Protection comes from the dust itself, molded to our skin like a perfect pie crust, cracking when we smile. We smile rarely and now the effort forces fault lines to fissure their way across our faces, seeking the path of least resistance. It hurts. I see Killen picking at his face, one giant scab that isn't ready to fall off yet. It's not that we never wash. We just never wash for long enough, always moving on our relentless quest. Plus, our dust jackets have their advantages: warding off frostbite; covering our scent.

We peel away layers of our wrappings as the Earth's surface heats. Flakes crumble away as piece by piece we reclaim ourselves from the dust. Virgin skin lies beneath, pure and naïve, ready to lose its innocence to the divine being. Skeins of blood vessels thread beneath the surface, blooming in the heat, flowering red all over our exposed surfaces.

Killen dances those first days, all spindly limbs crooking back and forth like a Halloween puppet, and how we laugh. We haven't stopped laughing since he first climbed that rise and we fell to our knees. Killen's jerky little body expresses everything we hope, but can't begin to put into words. Our faces speak to the future though: residual dirt, startled white streaks and ugly blotches of sun damage. A topographical map of our meagre expectations, our undying faith, our eventual undoing.

Days pass and the rays grow bolder, striking again and again at the dust clouds, finding their weaknesses. It is so beautiful it hurts. Shards of hot light fall to Earth's surface like a sheaf of arrows loosed from an avenging army. The dust gathers, safety in numbers, but the sun hunts it out and dismantles its dominion piece by piece.

Our rapture soon gives way to prickling apprehension, which in turn mutates into hot, searing dread. Killen is the first to fall, his childish exuberance creeping up behind him to take its revenge. We carry him between us, drip-feeding him brackish liquid, all we have.

Still we move. Any thought of not doing so has long since been eradicated, movement written deep into the fibers of our limbs as sure as the dust that coats our nostrils. The sun's triumphant return, a blaze of glory, is no reason to slow down. Quite the contrary. Petrified of stasis, we pay little heed to circadian cycles. Time slumbers in the dark, taking the sun down with it, so we make tracks at night, stealing like nocturnal prey. Gaining precious distance while our crisp faces gulp at the cool midnight air, rejuvenating.

Then one morning, the minutest sliver of color unfolds above us, unpicking the stitches that hold together the last shreds of the dust blanket. This must be what the forgottens called "blue". The sight of it shatters us. Killen falls again and rolls onto his back, gazing slack-jawed up at the sky as the rift of supernatural splendor stretches and distorts.

"No, Killen, come on," Iris rasps, pleading, dragging Killen by the wrists so his body leaves an undulating curve mark behind it in the dirt, a sand snake winding its way to shelter. But her eyes too are drawn skyward, and now we travel gazing up, seeking out that bleeding blue. It radiates west, a chasm of electric brightness luring us along with it.

Until finally, it shows us what was hidden from view under the dust. A city. It stands sentinel on the cusp of the dirt plains, smaller buildings bowing towards taller scrapers behind. Here is hope. Here is a goal. I don't dare breathe the notion to Iris, as she forges ahead, her slender shoulders pulled back, would-be fine blonde hair dreadlocked into submission by the dust. I watch, distracted, as it cascades down her back like a treacle waterfall. *She'll only want to pass through. Maybe even go around. We've skirted settlements for the best part of a year, after what happened in Gresham. Why would we want to change course again? Who knows what lies in wait.*

But she doesn't veer away as we expect. Killen and I dog her heels, unquestioning, and the cardboard cut-out horizon paves our way with lengthening shadows, a splaying grey crown of possibility. We dip our toes towards its shores, hesitant but needy.

"It's OK," says Iris. The emerging sun lit a fire in her eyes and it hasn't left them since, even though they water from the glare. She swells in its punishing glow like a ripening fruit. "We can. We can…." Her lips tremble as she unsticks them, and tears spill from her bloodshot eyes. She winces as they meander down the cracks in her brittle skin. It has to be her. Can only be Iris who speaks the word we have cold-shouldered for so long.

"The city. If we can reach it…we can…stop."

The word punctures the dusk, and what rushes through the hole it creates is all the bad juju, all the tension we have hauled along our path like dead weight. Sucked through the vacuum Iris pops in the choking bubble of our existence.

Killen's face steals the sun's fierce glow and beams it around on us, his feeble body rousing itself once more into motion. A brown-toothed keyboard grin embarks up his cheeks. If he can do it, so can we.

The dust clouds coalesce into frightened herds, and instead of driving them on, their long-time conspirator, the wind, harries them out of the way, herding them and penning them back. The way clears. The city ripples in the near-far, a mirage of potential, shimmering square and not-square in the dying light. We'll walk through the night once more.

Killen pushes back at his scabs, trying to make them part of him again. Iris and I scrape at the ground, desperate to claw back the protective coating to save from burning to the bone. But the dust turns its back on us now, adhering to the Earth, hardened to our plight. Too long we cursed it; now, too late, we lament its demise. Worse still, it takes the water with it, our canteens drying up as the dying dust sucks greedily at the dregs.

It becomes a cruel game of calculations and misjudgments. How fast can we go, without becoming dehydrated? How much liquid do we need, to get us to the next rise? Our skin blisters as, heat-addled and sun-blind, we fumble through the brilliance. Bargaining with time, the omnipresent substance of our nightmares. Its Cheshire Cat grin shining through the darkness now, watching impassive as we stumble on, seeking shade and anything with a payload of liquid we can tap. Scant opportunity.

"Iris?" Killen drops behind and my heart skips up its lethargic pace to a staccato beat. Not again. But if not him, I know it will be me. The numbness asks questions of my toes, my swollen ankles. Knees wobble with indecision. Once they decide, I won't get up again. The sun dries up the filthy puddles and arid desert catches fire, spreading across the plains like plague. Simple movement is no longer enough. We have to run.

The faster we go, the closer the settlement grows, tantalizing us with a prospect that has grown its own legs since Iris dared to utter it. The words spoken aloud shape our thoughts, govern our movements, put music into every step. If we reach the city, we can stop. We can stop. We can stop. We are a freight train, unrelenting in our progress. The blue draws my eyes upward, the city draws my body forward. I don't know if I sleep, the thoughts that possess my waking moments comprise my whole existence. Panic, falling upwards, driving my legs to move forward. Left, right. Left, right. If we reach the city, we can stop. We can stop. We can stop.

Iris falls. We're so close I can almost feel the cold concrete under my dry palms. She joins the ranks of Killen's ghosts, and I pull him by the wrist, grief a luxury neither of us can afford. Her words ring through the blue as clear as if she were still running with us.

If we reach the city.

We can stop. We can stop. We can....

When we reach the city.

"Dust Jackets"

KATY MADGWICK is a private English tutor, baby swim teacher, and freelance writer, living in the northeast of England with two small humans, one larger one, and an unruly sprocker puppy called Skye. She holds an MA in Modern and Contemporary Literature, and has a background in blogging. "Dust Jackets" is her first published short story.

She says: "I began writing 'Dust Jackets' without knowing where the story was heading, but my enduring affection for post-apocalyptic literature combined with acute climate-change anxiety shaped the story as I wrote. It underwent a few structural alterations before I was happy with it, and only after submission did I realise the story also touches on my recurring preoccupation with isolationism versus community, a theme that emerges from almost everything I write—whether or not I intend it to."

Phillip Sandberg

Hail Celsius

IT WAS A PLEASURE TO BURN. Of course, it was. A pleasure so enveloping I felt nothing for anything else.

It was a pleasure to watch the kindling and newsprint pump and haemorrhage that pure white smoke up until the point of combustion, to see the licks of flame eat that tee-pee of larger twigs stacked in the layer above, and to smell the eucalyptus oil from the woodpile's split-log crown as fire singed the hairy fibres of bark before taking hold of the hardwood and its core of gummy sap.

It was a pleasure to watch the sparks pop and spawn across the carpet, to the curtains, to the rest of the house, my father's house.

It was my father who taught me how to build a fire, a proper fire, and he was a good teacher. Leathery and beetroot-red from too much sun and too much rum, he would say any idiot can pour petrol on a pile of logs, but if you were stuck in the middle of nowhere you needed to know how to build a fire that would keep you warm, keep you fed, and get you rescued.

He would build his fires at sunset, before the evening had time to lay down its first film of moisture. The piled wood flared and flamed into the sky, as if trying to join the Southern Cross and that infinity of orbs burning across the night. Once reduced to embers, the ash-shells of trunks and branches would glow with veins of pulsing orange.

Into those hot coals my father would place a tin full of water to boil for his coffee or tea. He'd then wrap potatoes, carrots and swedes in aluminium foil, driving them into the embers with a stick. While the vegetables roasted, he would use a cast iron pan to fry the rabbits, their hairless, headless bodies splayed and spitting in the sizzling butter.

To catch the rabbits, we used ferrets. Weasel-faced flashes of fur, they had sharp teeth, sharp claws and a sharp stench. Down the rabbit-holes they would dart, chasing the terrified vermin out into the nets we had staked over the holes of the warren. It was my job to free the rabbits from the nets and shove them into hessian bags where they would jerk and kick like foetuses choking on dust in some dried-out womb.

Later, we would twist and twist their little heads around until their necks snapped and all expression froze in their little brown eyes. Then we would skin and gut them. Skins would be dried and sold for the fur lining of motorcycle gloves. We would keep some meat for ourselves and the rest we would sell to the owner of the pub in town. The guts would go to the ferrets. Sometimes the tiny rabbit hearts would still be beating.

I would feel my heart beat, too, every time a rabbit escaped my grip.

"Look at you! You're fucking hopeless," my father would yell. "That's money running out the door, dickhead."

His anger was subject to the "rum ratio." The more he drank, the less he spoke and the greater the bruising on my body.

As well as lighting fires, my father knew how to put them out. Along with his brother, he joined the local fire brigade. At first it was to "impress the sheilas," but after marrying my mum, and summer after summer of charred paddocks, smoking farmhouses and incinerated livestock, his motivations became more existential.

One summer, just before Christmas, the neighbour's kids and I climbed on top of our shed to watch the distant specks of my father, uncle and the other volunteers as they faced a fire-front bulldozing its way through the wheat fields on the outskirts of town. It had leapt from the bush and the scrub of the surrounding hills bringing with it clouds of smoke and embers. As the sky became dark and the sun a blood-red disc, blackened gum leaves fell around us like tiny, charred skydivers.

A change in the wind and some quick back-burning spared the more vulnerable houses before the tankers ran dry. My father and my uncle and the others were heroes.

My mum kept an old picture of them in the house. It was all scratched and sepia, taken at the Brigades State Games, before I was born. My father and uncle are standing at the front, their brass-buttoned, double-breasted coats kept in check by big leather belts with thick square buckles. Instead of helmets with numbers on them, each man's coat is sewn with a nametag while the hats they wear look borrowed from the Salvation Army. My father holds the nozzle of a fire hose. Its length is wrapped around a spool suspended between two wagon wheels. It looks like some flaccid piece of artillery.

My uncle was a reasonable man, to a point. He said he had joined the brigade out of a respect for fire. He hated what it did to people, animals, communities, the way it monstered across the landscape leaving nothing growing or grazing, poisoning the water, burning the lungs of children. But, to him it was also part of the natural order of things. The Aborigines had the right idea, he would say. They used fire to shape the bush, to limit the destruction, to bring forth the seeds of renewal. We had a lot to learn.

He caught me in the shed one day. Opposing armies of plastic soldiers lay before me and I was the god of war. The spray-on, aerosol lubricant was mostly hydrocarbons and with a spark from a lighter became a poor man's flamethrower. Platoon after platoon of marines boiled and melted before me and if you picked up one of the larger enlisted men, the plastic would drip onto the troops below with the sound of a science-fiction laser gun. I loved the smell of WD-40 in the morning.

My uncle was upset. I thought it was because they were my cousin's toy soldiers. After putting out the flames, he told my father. After that, I was beaten.

My cousin seemed to get over his loss. In time, he also joined the fire brigade. He rose quickly through the ranks at State Headquarters becoming the face of the service on the news bulletins. Looking grim and crisp in his white shirt with blue epaulets, he would look straight into the camera urging viewers to immediately enact their fire plans. Tickers would scroll across the screen below him listing nearby towns in imminent danger. My aunt was very proud.

She was also considered very glamourous, especially for a town the size of ours. She loved floral dresses, horseracing carnivals, champagne and cigarettes. Her favourite day of the year was the Melbourne Cup holiday. Feathery fascinator in her hair, she would stride in unfaltering high-heels toward the bookies at the track, look them in the eye and lay down her bets. When the last nag of the day had crossed the finish line, she would jubilantly wave gloved hands full of banknotes and invite the crowd back to our house to dance and drink and smoke.

She burnt my eyelid with a celebratory Marlboro. The smouldering rod crumpled as she rushed from our shed and her hand collided with my face. Amongst my screaming and my aunt's cursing, the shed door swung open. Inside I saw my father pulling up his trousers. So did a yard full of people and my mum. Weeks later, after long silences broken by raging arguments and assaults, my mother filled one of my father's spare tyres with mower fuel, put it over her shoulders and set it alight like she'd seen the South Africans do on the news.

I don't know who it was who said time heals all wounds. At the Christmas dinner, all those years later, I still had the scar on my eyelid, the arthritis in my back still reminded me of my father's fists and my mum's ashes were still bottled in their ceramic jail cell. Why wouldn't I tie them all up, make a proper fire in the loungeroom and burn them all to hell?

The police and ambulance crew have wrapped me in foil. I feel like one of my father's roast vegetables. They tell me I will be kept under guard until I am charged, that I will be likely refused bail, that a judge will come to hold a bedside hearing at the hospital, when we reach the city.

"Hail Celsius"

PHILLIP SANDBERG is an editor and journalist in New South Wales, Australia. He is also the Publisher and part-owner of *Content+Technology* magazine, a trade title for media professionals in Australia, New Zealand, and Southeast Asia. His early career was peppered with obscure poetry journals, underground publications, and spoken-word performance poetry. "Hail Celsius" is his first published short story.

He says: "That opening line from *Fahrenheit 451* presented me with two options—a story drawing on the experience of growing up in the fire-prone tinderbox of the Australian bush, or an exploration of the tragic world of tanning salon addiction. I chose the former."

Honorable Mentions

We received hundreds of submissions to this year's Literary Taxidermy Short Story Competition, and many impressed both early readers and final judges. In the end many good stories were turned away. The following stories all made it to the last round of selection. Keep an eye out for these writers. We're confident you'll see their work in the future.

Therese Adams, "Save the Children"
Jules Van Arden, "Polilla"
Martin Brennan, "Trailblazers"
Kale Brown, "City in the Sky"
Gilbert Ben Brynildsen, "The Black Hot Sauce"
Grey C. C., "Stowaways"
Stephanie Clark, "The Weight of Ash"
Ilana Conway, "The Pizza"
Michele Conyngham, "Sonnet 45 Degrees"
Seonaid Louise Cook, *"Walpurgisnacht"*
Seonaid Louise Cook, "Wild Swimming"
Shauna Crampsie, "An Exhaustive Cycle"
Nicole S. Entin, "The Divine Grill"
T.Y. Euliano, "The Intern"
Michelle Henry, "Petting Bumblebees"
Morgan Jeffery, "Painted Red"
Meredith Jelbart, "Of Fire and Flood"
Molly S. Kelash, "No Woman No Cry"

Mel Kennard, "Children of Summer"

Michael Lynch, *"Eta Aquariids"*

Sean McConville, *"Rodentia Mutatis"*

Jeremy McDonald, "The Westering Bulb"

Janna Tinley Miller, "Under the Grey"

Lucy Sarah Moor Tyndall, "The Gaslighting"

Cassandra Parkin, "The Only Things That Happen Are the Things inside Your Head"

Kate Phimy, "Remember Remember"

David Prysock, "Proxies"

Eric Reitan, "Phoenix without Fire"

Rick Shingler, "The Crusade of the Hellfire Kid"

Barbara Thompson, "Pull the Plug and Jump"

Alana Turner, "The Cleansing"

Seth Venable, "Sunburn"

Cecily Jane Vermote, "Sounds in the Dark"

Barbara Young, "Utopolis"

Sara E. Zeller, "Burning Bright"

This Year's Judges

Given our desire for submissions to span genres, we assembled a group of professional writers and editors from all walks of the literary life. The judges for this year's competition included a poet, a speculative fiction writer, a memoirist, a playwright, a mystery writer, a food writer, a fantasy writer, and a creative non-fiction writer. They had a challenging task, separating not only wheat from chaff, but wheat from wheat, and we are grateful for their enthusiastic and perspicacious participation.

Catherine Barnett is the author of three collections of poems: *Human Hours* (2018), *The Game of Boxes* (2012), and *Into Perfect Spheres Such Holes Are Pierced* (2004). Her honors include a Whiting Award, a Guggenheim Fellowship, and the James Laughlin Award from the Academy of American Poets. She has published widely in journals and magazines, including *The New Yorker*, *The Kenyon Review*, and *The Washington Post*. Barnett teaches in the graduate and undergraduate programs at New York University. She has degrees from Princeton University, where she has taught in the Lewis Center for the Arts, and from the MFA Program for Writers at Warren Wilson College.

Kelley Eskridge is a fiction writer, essayist, and screenwriter. She is the author of the New York Times Notable novel *Solitaire*, a finalist for the Nebula, Endeavour, and Spectrum awards. The short stories in her collection *Dangerous Space* include an Astraea prize winner and finalists for the Nebula and Tiptree awards. Eskridge's story "Alien Jane" was adapted for an episode of the SciFi channel series *Welcome to Paradox*. Her film *OtherLife* (2017) is currently streaming on Netflix. She is a former vice president of Wizards of the Coast, the company responsible for the collectible trading games *Magic*™ and *Pokémon*™. She earns her keep as a corporate learning professional, as well as an independent editor with an international client list of established and emerging writers. She lives in Seattle with her wife, novelist Nicola Griffith.

Christine S. O'Brien grew up in New York City and Beverly Hills. She earned a BA in English at UC Berkeley and holds a Double MFA from Saint Mary's College in Nonfiction and Fiction, where she was awarded Saint Mary's Agnes Butler Scholarship for Literary Excellence. Her lyric essay "Fish" appeared in *The Seneca Review*, and her short story, "Cullen Farm," appeared in *The Slush Pile Magazine*. Her essay, "Cul de Sac," received Honorable Mention in *Glimmer Train*'s 2014 Short Story Award for New Writers. She is currently a part-time lecturer in the English Composition Department at Saint Mary's College. Her memoir, *CRAVE*, sold out of its first printing in only 2 ½ weeks.

Brian Parks is an American playwright, journalist, and editor. He lives in New York City and served as the Arts & Culture editor at *The Village Voice*, as well as Chairman of the Obie Awards. As a playwright, Brian has produced works that are noted for their dark comedy and fast pace. Best known for his play "Americana Absurdum" (which consists of the two shorter plays, "Vomit & Roses" and "Wolverine Dream"), his other works include "Goner," "Suspicious Package," "Out of the Way," "The Invitation," and "Imperial Fizz." "Americana Absurdum" was honored with the Best Writing award at the 1997 New York International Fringe Festival and a Scotsman Fringe First

Award at the 2000 Edinburgh Festival Fringe. He is currently Senior Editor at *4Columns*, a website of arts criticism aimed at a general audience.

Michael Pronko is a mystery writer, essayist, and teacher, born in Kansas City, but living and writing in Tokyo for the past twenty years. He has published three award-winning collections of essays: *Beauty and Chaos: Essays on Tokyo*; *Motions and Moments: More Essays on Tokyo*; and *Tokyo's Mystery Deepens*. His award-winning mystery novels *The Last Train* and *The Moving Blade* (as well as the forthcoming *Japan Hand*) feature Detective Hiroshi Shimizu who investigates white collar crime in Tokyo. He writes regularly for many publications, including *The Japan Times*, *Newsweek Japan*, *Jazznin*, *Jazz Colo[u]rs*, and *Artscape Japan*; and runs his own website, *Jazz in Japan*. He is a professor of American Literature at Meiji Gakuin University where he teaches seminars in contemporary novels and film adaptations.

Becky Selengut is a cooking teacher, private chef, not-so-private comedian, and a prolific food writer. Her books include *The Washington Local and Seasonal Cookbook* (2008); *Good Fish: Sustainable Seafood Recipes from the Pacific Coast* (2011 and 2018); *Shroom: Mind-Bendingly Good Recipes for Cultivated and Wild Mushrooms* (2014); *Not One Shrine: Two Food Writers Devour Tokyo* (2016); and *How to Taste: The Curious Cook's Handbook to seasoning and balance, from umami to acid and beyond* (2018). In her spare time she co-hosts *Look Inside This Book Club*, a NSFW comedy podcast with Matthew Amster-Burton that discusses the free Kindle preview—and ONLY the preview—of bestselling books, usually while sipping Pinot Grigio.

Nisi Shawl is an African-American writer, editor, and journalist. She is best known as an author of fantasy and science fiction who writes and teaches about how fantastic fiction might reflect real-world diversity of gender, sexual orientation, race, colonialism, physical ability, age, and other sociocultural factors. Her debut novel, *Everfair*, was a 2016 Nebula Awards finalist, and her short stories have appeared in *Asimov's Science Fiction*, the *Infinite Matrix*, *Strange Horizons*, *Semiotext(e)* and numerous other magazines and anthologies. Her story collection Filter House was one of two winners of the 2008 James Tiptree, Jr. Award. During the ceremony, she was crowned with the Tiptree tiara and given a plaque, a check, a pie, and a ceramic sculpture of a duck.

Melora Wolff received her BA from Brown University and her MFA from Columbia University. Her essays and prose poems appear widely in journals and anthologies, including *The Normal School*, *Salmagundi*, *The New York Times*, and *Best American Fantasy*. Her prose has received Special Mentions in Nonfiction from The Pushcart Prizes, several Notable Essay citations in *Best American Essays*, and the Thomas A. Wilhelmus Award in Short Prose. She is the author of *The Parting*, a collection of magical realist flash fictions. She lives and writes in Saratoga Springs, New York and teaches on the faculty of Skidmore College.

You, Too, May Become a Taxidermist!

All of us at Regulus Press wish to extend our thanks and appreciation to everyone who participated in the 2019 Literary Taxidermy Short Story Competition. Your enthusiasm and commitment far exceeded our expectations—as did the *overwhelming* number of story submissions we received.

If you didn't participate this year and are coming to this collection of stories new to the idea of literary taxidermy, we hope you've enjoyed what you've found. And if you're a writer, we encourage you—the present reader—to become a future literary taxidermist.

This is our second year running the competition, and we're hoping to do it again, so we're looking for writers, both amateur and professional, to stitch together new and imaginative stories. The competition is your chance to get your hands dirty and join the growing community of literary taxidermists.

For the latest on the competition (and to learn more about the possibilities of literary taxidermy), visit:

www.literarytaxidermy.com

We look forward to seeing what you come up with!

About the Editors

Mark Malamud is a tail-end baby-boomer and master dogsbody. His collection of short stories, *The Gymnasium*, established the idea of literary taxidermy. His novel, *Float the Pooch*—which pits David Bowie against Stanley Kubrick against a background of alien invasion, future sex, and Yom Kippur—is widely unread.

Paul Van Zwalenburg is a writer and editor living in the Pacific Northwest. Originally from Hawaii, he spends an inordinate amount of time trying to turn his two children into surfers, despite the near total absence of decent waves anywhere along the Cascadia Coast.

Other Books from Regulus Press

A Pocketful of Fish

A seaworthy celebration of dubious poetry, bringing together three previously-published collections of verse: *Swimming through the Darkness* (1974), *Roe Roe Roe Your Boat* (1978), and *Will You Hold My Breath* (1994). Recipient of numerous accolades including the National Poetry Award in 1974, and the Boating Association *Truite d'Or* in 1980. Poetry by Choo 3T Fish.

Against the Bar

An anthology of literary taxidermy based on the first and last lines of *The Thin Man* by Dashiell Hammett. Award-winning stories from the 2018 Literary Taxidermy Short Story Competition.

The Gymnasium

Nineteen tales of melancholy and wonder created by "re-stuffing" what goes in-between the opening and closing lines of classic works by Milan Kundera, Philip K. Dick, Thomas Wolfe, Ian Fleming, and others. The inspiration for the Literary Taxidermy Short Story Competition. Short stories by Mark Malamud.

On the Orient Express

A daring act of narrative appropriation, modification, and reinterpretation of an original text by Agatha Christie. By altering an event early in Christie's novel—there is no murder—the remaining text must re-adjust to accommodate the absence of the crime. The result is a transformation of the original novel into something entirely different: an expression of redemption rather than of revenge. A "re-novel" by Mark Malamud.

www.ingramcontent.com/pod-product-compliance
Lightning Source LLC
Chambersburg PA
CBHW020943180626
46814CB00003B/944